SWAY with the WIND

A Prequel Novella

Content Warning

Books in the Desert of Dreams Series address many sensitive but important topics. This book includes the topics of bullying; historical events of the 1960s; racism and classism; dealing with death and trauma (generational and situational); and depression.

If you or someone you know is struggling with their mental health or is in crisis, please reach out for help. In the US, you can call or text the National Suicide and Crisis Lifeline at 988.

SWAY with the WIND

A Prequel Novella

Desert of Dreams Series

AMANDA LAPERA

ADAMO PRESS
Aliso Viejo, Calif.

Sway with the Wind, A Prequel Novella
(*Desert of Dreams Series*)

This is a work of fiction. References to historical events and places are used fictitiously. Names, characters, places, and events portrayed in this book are products of the author's imagination. Any resemblance to actual persons, living or dead, events, or locales is entirely coincidental.

Copyright © 2025 by Amanda LaPera. All rights reserved.

First edition

Published by Adamo Press, 27068 La Paz Rd, Suite 102, Aliso Viejo, California 92656. Printed in the United States of America. No part of this book may be used or stored in any electronic form or reproduced in any manner whatsoever without prior written permission except in the case of brief quotations embodied in critical articles and reviews. Scanning, uploading, or distributing this book without permission is theft. No permission is granted for use with any AI system or program. Thank you for supporting the author by buying an authorized copy of this book. To schedule a virtual or in-person event with the author, or to inquire about discounts for bulk purchases, contact us at info@adamopress.com or www.adamopress.com.

Library of Congress Control Number: 2025950747

Publisher's Cataloging-in-Publication Data

Names: LaPera, Amanda, 1978- author.
Title: Sway with the wind / Amanda LaPera.
Description: Aliso Viejo, Calif. : Adamo Press, [2025] | Series: Desert of dreams series ; prequel. | At foot of title on cover: Trauma, resilience, hope. | Audience: Young adult.
Identifiers: LCCN: 2025950747 | ISBN: 9781965660072 (hardcover) | 9781965660065 (paperback) | 9781965660058 (eBook)
Subjects: LCSH: Teenage girls--Psychology--Fiction. | Teenagers--Family relationships--Fiction. | Small cities--Fiction. | Lake Los Angeles (Calif.)--Fiction. | Mojave Desert--Fiction. | Hope--Fiction. | Resilience (Personality trait)--Fiction. | Healing--Fiction. | Self-esteem--Fiction. | Self-reliance--Fiction. | Bildungsromans. | Romance fiction. | BISAC: YOUNG ADULT FICTION / Coming of Age. | YOUNG ADULT FICTION / Girls & Women.
Classification: LCC: PS3612.A5894 D370 2025 | DDC: 813/.6--dc23

Cover design by Fiona Jayde Media

Dedicated to those whose lives have been affected by uncontrollable change

TABLE OF CONTENTS

1 Lovejoy	1
2 Quartz	10
3 Dealing Differently	18
4 The Ranch	25
5 Sienna	32
6 Times Have Changed	41
7 Rough Patch	48
8 Outlaws	57
9 Chasing Dreams	65
10 Premonition	73
11 Earth and Sky Alight	80
12 Inferno	87
13 Broken	90
14 Like Magic	95
15 Secrecy	102
16 Proposals	109
17 The Crux of It	118
18 Taking Flight	127
Epilogue	135
Author's Note	138
Acknowledgements	139
Discussion Questions	140
About the Author	141
Also by the Author	142

1

Lovejoy

Beverly Hills, California, November 1959

THERE WOULD BE NO LOVE nor joy in the town of Lovejoy. Not as far as eleven-year-old Anne Dougherty was concerned. And nothing on the nearby desert ranch to look forward to except her grandpa. Even that was debatable.

She shoved her luggage in the trunk and slammed it shut. A logo on the side of the car read: Children's Home Society of California. She slid into the back of the car and, with a steady beat, kicked the seat in front of her.

The social worker, a poodle-cut brunette with magenta lipstick, could've passed as Lucille Ball's much older sister. She even smoked the same Philip Morris cigarettes. Mildred—just call me Midge, she'd said in court—shifted the car into drive.

Anne turned and kneeled on the vinyl back seat to stare out the rear window. The white shutters and colonial styled columns on her house grew smaller, as did the other elegant two-story estates with their manicured lawns. The palm-tree-lined streets with ornate street lamps disappeared, along with every friend she'd ever made. Even the family cat, made nervous by all the activity, had run off days earlier and couldn't be found.

Anne faced forward, tucked her long dark hair behind her headband, and resumed the rhythmic kicking of the seat in front of her.

"You know," Midge said as she peered at Anne in the rearview mirror, "accepting a thing that can't be changed is better than fighting it."

When Midge redirected her eyes on the road, Anne crossed her arms and stuck her tongue out at her. All of Los Angeles faded away. Even the sky was a hazy gray.

On the highway, the San Gabriel Mountains loomed larger and their purple hue turned brown. Anne kept kicking the seat.

"Would you knock it off, please?" Midge asked. "It wouldn't kill you to be polite."

Kill you. Bad choice of words. Midge bit her lower lip and didn't say another word about the kicking that continued for the rest of the drive.

On the other side of the mountains, Anne's legs got tired and she slouched back. The sky transformed into a vibrant blue as they crested the mountain pass and began their descent. No buildings in sight. The wide-open vista presented nothing but disappointment.

Specks in the desert landscape took shape as they drew closer. She hadn't visited her grandpa for several years. Back then, her mom pointed out the spiky Joshua trees—how could settlers have mistaken these for palm trees? —and explained how the hardy succulents survived with little to no rain. Scrubby brush became scrubbier as the car turned onto a mostly empty two-lane road. When the road turned to corrugated dirt, Anne's bottom bumped on the back seat. This wasn't the path she remembered taking with her parents.

"He's way out here," Midge said. "We're getting close, though." She held the steering wheel with one hand and a hand-drawn map with the other.

Anne pressed her face against the cool glass. Midge slowed to avoid tumbleweeds that rolled across the road and into the fields. Anne's stomach sank. The closer they got to the ranch, the harder reality hit. Why couldn't she have been in the car with her parents that night, instead of being dragged out here to die?

Dust kicked up behind the car, blocking out the sun. They crossed railroad tracks and kept going until they neared a huge mound of rocks, Lovejoy Buttes, namesake of the town.

The car came to a stop at an intersection. On both sides were alfalfa fields, the only green as far as Anne could see. Satisfied that no one else was foolish enough to be driving out there, Midge urged the car forward. The dirt road curved. A few houses—at least half a mile from one another—dotted the landscape, interspersed with green farms, desert fields, fenced-off ranches, and more desert fields.

Her other grandparents were pushing eighty. "Too old to raise a child," they had told the judge. Couldn't they have hired a nanny? Why send her away to certain misery on a ranch in the Antelope Valley, way out in the California Mojave Desert?

She was never a bad kid—did her piano lessons and ballet lessons, made her bed, and curtsied when called upon to do so. Maybe she would've had better luck in foster care back home. Not allowed. "Better she live with family," the judge's words echoed in her head.

As they came around the bend, a familiar sight came into view: the wooden split rail fence—pieced together from old railroad ties. Beyond that, the pear orchard with its mature trees in perfect rows. The car paused under the gateway. The sign atop had text branded with a hot iron: Hoffman Ranch.

"Look familiar?" Midge asked.

Anne nodded and they drove through the open gate. The car bumped along the ridges and dipped on the potholes along the uneven path. The tires crunched along the scattered gravel.

In the distance was a corral with a couple of horses and a rundown looking barn. Buttes served as the backdrop for the ranch. The car came to a stop in front of the old, wood-shingled, single-story house. A cloud of dirt enveloped the car. After it settled, Midge hitched a large purse up on her shoulder and opened the door. Anne stayed put.

Wind whistled and Midge held her hand on her hair. A gust pushed her back a step. Three cattle dogs sprinted toward her, barking. She hurried back into the car and slammed the door. The dogs ran in circles and barked at them.

Anne stifled a laugh.

Midge panted and slowed her breathing. "All right," she said. "If the dogs don't alert him, I'll honk the horn. Until then, we'll wait in here."

Sure enough, Anne's lanky grandpa sauntered out in jeans, boots, and a button-up plaid flannel. A big belt buckle sat over his lean belly, and he wore a bandana over his nose and mouth like a robber. When he slipped it down, he was clean-shaven. He removed his cowboy hat, revealing short wavy brown hair, and waved at them.

Midge rolled down her window.

"How do you do? Name's Andy." He bent over to peer at the back seat then stood and smiled. "Sorry about them. Buck, Dusty, and Jesse get a little excited. We don't often get visitors in fancy cars." He whistled at the dogs. They sat beside him, wagging their tails. "Even though we don't raise cattle here, cattle dogs are useful to have around. Would you like to come in?"

"Yes, I have some papers for you to sign." Midge cautiously exited the car. She opened the door for Anne while Andy collected the bags from the trunk.

Anne stepped out into the blinding brightness. Her bare legs were hit by a cool gust of wind that flung grits of sand at her skin. She held down the hem of her knee-length dress as her black and white saddle shoes crossed the dirt yard—by the time she reached the front porch, they were covered in dust, her hair was tangled, and her arms had goosebumps. It wasn't nearly this cold back in LA. Is this what her mom meant by the High Desert? A sign back on the highway had said 3,000 feet above sea level.

It took a while for Anne's eyes to adjust to the dim interior of the house. The air was dank, the carpet old and worn down, the furniture a mixture of mint green and various mismatched shades of wood.

"Coffee?" Andy asked.

"Tea please," Midge said. "If it's not too much trouble."

"No trouble at all, ma'am." Andy set a kettle on the stove and turned on the burner.

The three took a seat at the oak kitchen table. Well-worn nicks and scratches indicated the sturdy table was likely older than any of them.

Midge unwound the string on a manila envelope and slid out a stack of papers.

"The adoption papers," she said, and uncapped a pen. "I'll need a couple of signatures from you. These are your copies... and here is Anne's birth certificate." She lowered her voice to a whisper. "The death certificates are here as well."

Anne got up and crossed the room. A China cabinet and hutch held a collection of dishes that didn't look much nicer than the ones used every day at her house, although these were outlined with gold and roses, an odd choice for a fifty-something man living by himself. Judging by the layers of dust on the shelves, maybe they hadn't been used since before her grandma died, which was long before Anne was born.

She paced into the living room. Carved wooden legs supported the sofa, upholstered in the mint green. Crocheted doilies covered the arms—another odd choice for her grandpa. The sofa hardly looked used. The recliner, on the other hand, stationed in front of the television, had done more than its fair share.

Anne moved to the hallway where she studied the black-and-white family portraits that lined the walls. Her grandpa appeared at the end of the hallway.

"I'm glad you're here, Anne," he said. "Suppose you've had a long day already. Would you like to see your room?"

She nodded and followed him to the second of three bedrooms, the one where her parents slept the last time the three of them visited. Inside, a four-poster bed was made, a patchwork quilt spread across the top. Another quilt, pale green with pink roses, hung on the wall. A dark walnut dresser with an attached mirror and a writing desk lined the other wall. Beside the bed, a small pedestal table supported a lamp with a dusty cream lampshade. The outer curtains, made of dark, dusty velvet, were drawn open and sunlight streamed through the yellowed inner lace curtains.

"It's not much," he said. "But you can make it your own." He went out and returned with her luggage, which he placed next to a large wooden chest at the foot of the bed. "That's your trunk. You've got a couple of boxes in the closet as well. I brought that all up here for you if you remember."

She didn't want to remember. The last time he visited her in LA was a terribly unpleasant day, everyone and everything covered in black. The sight of the trunk that held her dolls and books and playthings pinched at her heart.

The kettle whistled. Rather than linger in misery, she followed her grandpa back out.

He brought three teacups and a bowl of sugar to the table.

Midge thanked him and asked about the ranch.

He leaned back in his chair. "Got chickens and sheep and a few goats—great for the weeds—along with the pear trees, and the horses and dogs, of course. A few cats here and there manage to play a pretty good keep-away from the coyotes."

Midge blanched at the mention of coyotes. "Do you get much rain?"

He shook his head. "Afraid not. Rely on irrigation mostly. Lovejoy Springs flowed until the Tehachapi quake a few years back. Lovejoy Lake and the groundwater have been good enough to keep us watered, even when the weather hasn't. Can't say the same for some of the folks living further out."

They sipped their tea, each one waiting for the other to speak. Anne kept her elbows off the table and took another spoonful of sugar. Her tea at home wasn't nearly as bitter.

"Where will she be enrolled in school?" Midge asked. She, too, spooned more sugar.

"Nice school just up that way a mile," he said, gesturing out the window. "Wilsona Elementary School opened back in 1915. Looks a lot better now than back then. Alice and I sent all our kids there. Course it wasn't around when I grew up."

"How long have you been here?"

"Born here in 1903. My folks homesteaded in the 1890s. When Alice and I got married, we stuck around to help them out." He sighed. "The '30s were rough."

Midge nodded. "The Great Depression left a mark on us all."

"Not just that. I lost my parents and wife along with a baby in a span of five years."

"I'm sorry to hear that." Midge leaned forward, concern across her face. "You raised your kids on your own?"

"All four of them." He glanced at Anne. "Lucky enough to have another go at it."

No one said anything for a while and instead focused on sipping their tea.

Anne's stomach rumbled. She covered it with her hands.

"Heard that," her grandpa said. "Let me get you some toast and marmalade. Afraid I wasn't sure if you'd be up in time for lunch."

Midge stood. "I best be headed back. It was a pleasure to see you again, Mr. Hoffman. If you need anything at all, my card is in that packet."

Anne gave her a polite hug goodbye on the porch. Before stepping back into her car, Midge scanned the desert landscape and turned back to Anne with sad eyes. She plastered on a smile, waved goodbye, and took off in the way she'd come.

A dust cloud followed in her wake.

If it weren't for the bitter cold wind, Anne would've stayed outside and watched the car—and her hopes and dreams—disappear into the distance.

2

Quartz

ANNE'S GRANDPA WORKED on the ranch with his helpers for the rest of the day. It was already dark when he came back inside and went straight to the kitchen pantry.

"Jar of peaches, pears, can of chili or baked beans, some corn, cereal." He opened the refrigerator and freezer. "Frozen peas and chicken. Got a pot pie in there." He turned to Anne. "How does that sound? Chicken pot pie."

"Yes, please." Anne nodded. The toast and marmalade had held her over until dinner but wouldn't last until breakfast. "May I help?"

"I got it from here. Want to watch TV while it cooks?"

He turned the dial to the Saturday night Western show, *Bonanza*—in black-and-white. *Bonanza*, Anne's favorite Western, was the first TV series that aired in color. She had viewed the first few episodes with her parents on their new color television. She blinked at the TV. Why wasn't the color working?

Oh. Grandpa didn't have money for a new TV. Why couldn't she have brought hers over? What would happen to her house and all the furniture?

Cowboys rode their horses across the fuzzy, snowy TV screen.

Anne sat on the carpet close to the TV, then lay down on her belly, and rested on her elbows. After a few minutes, she hardly noticed the lack of color.

With the pot pie in the oven, her grandpa joined her in the living room. He settled into his recliner and kicked up his feet.

Right at the climax of the show, the buzzer in the kitchen went off. As soon as the commercials hit, they set up two TV trays to enjoy dinner during the last segment of the show.

"What did you think?" He wiped his mouth.

"Exciting," she said. "Can't wait for next week."

While they cleaned the dishes together—he washed, she dried—he spoke to her about the film industry, something she knew quite a bit about because of her dad, a big-time producer.

"Did you know they film out here in the desert? Watch for the buttes and Joshua trees. You'll recognize them sometimes in the background."

She nodded, thankful that her grandpa didn't repeat the story of how her parents met. Her dad, twice her mom's age at the time, met her while he visited a Western set on behalf of his parents' production company. Her mom, watching from a distance, had caught his eye. He convinced her, barely eighteen, to wear a prairie dress and "star" as an extra in the film.

Thinking of her parents hurt. She held back her tears until she'd towel-dried the last dish. She thanked her grandpa for dinner and ran to her room to cry. She sobbed into her pillow where no one, not even God, could hear.

There weren't any girls her age living on the neighboring farms, and very few in her grade at the small school, but Anne preferred to stick to herself anyways. After three months at her new school, Anne had come to fully accept that her fellow students were nothing like those in LA. The kids here, a rough and tumble group, helped their parents on farms and on ranches after school—no ballet or piano lessons. Most of them hung out at nearby Lovejoy Lake, and fished for catfish whenever given the chance.

She wasn't motivated to walk to the small lake, because she didn't care for fishing and had no one to talk to. Plus, why admit there was anything good about being stuck out there?

Another reason is that she did have an early memory, one of her earliest, of fishing with her mom at the lake. It was a pleasant memory and for that reason it was a dreadfully painful one. This is why she pretended the lake didn't exist and wandered off into her own head whenever it was mentioned.

Anne didn't help her grandpa on the ranch, either. Instead, in the chilly late winter wind, she clambered over Lovejoy Buttes, tearing up her jeans and scuffing up her sneakers. Her hands roughened from gripping the loose quartz that crumbled in her palms as she scrambled around.

Wind whipped at her while she examined all sides of the buttes—save for the lake surrounded by cattails and scrubby trees—an anomaly in the vast emptiness of the desert, which she ignored. Instead, she longed for the far side of the purple-hued San Gabriel Mountains, the coastal side, back home.

One day, she climbed all the way up, over boulders bigger than a horse. Huffing and puffing, she rested at the top, which afforded a grand view of the nothingness that surrounded her. The sunshine was blinding so Anne stared down at the ground. The rocks by her feet were streaked with sparkling quartz. Whenever she moved her head, the sunlight made them shimmer.

A squawk overhead caught her attention. She squinted against the bright sun. A majestic hawk soaring across the bright blue sky circled overhead.

Anne reached down, grabbing a rock that fit nicely in her palm. She pulled back her arm and launched it into the air at the large bird of prey, too high for her aim. The rock struck a boulder and loose granite broke off, sharp projectiles jetting out in every direction. Another rock, another throw. Another and another until Anne's hair stuck to her sweaty forehead.

The hawk eyed her and kept its distance.

When she tired of the target practice, Anne flopped down onto the gritty dirt and hugged her knees. She wiped her face, surprised to find it streaked with tears.

The hawk perched twenty feet away, on a large boulder atop the highest peak of the buttes. It faced her and cocked its head to the side before shaking its wings and fluffing its neck feathers—a beautiful creature.

With a burst of energy, Anne jumped to her feet, scooped up a handful of quartz, sprinted closer and viciously threw the rocks at the hawk. It spread its wings and effortlessly soared over her head, circling twice, then disappeared into the far distance.

After school, Anne stopped at the foot of the buttes. The winter wind whipped her hair out of her ponytail and stung her ears and nose. Dirt kicked up in the distance and funneled a bit before dissipating in the air, resuming its place on the desert floor.

She opened her flowered tin lunchbox and loaded it with a bunch of rocks—quartz, rose, sandy brown, some streaked with fool's gold—and latched it shut. With the rocks inside, the lunchbox was too heavy to carry one-handed. She hugged it close to her chest and jogged to the edge of her grandpa's property. In the shade behind the barn, she examined her arsenal.

Rocks in both hands, she approached a cluster of Joshua Trees—tall, spiky, and older than her. She threw one rock after another. A direct hit to the Dr. Seuss-style twisted succulents. After a dozen rocks, she managed to hit a flower, a creamy white cluster of blooms, one of the earliest of the season.

"You stupid, stupid tree," Anne yelled. "I hate you."

With renewed determination, she gathered more loose rocks, got closer and took vengeful aim at the flower. She screamed and cried as she launched the projectiles. Eventually, the top of the flower bent, snapped off and dropped to the ground.

Marching over to it she pounced, stomped, and twisted her feet, smashing the firm buds. She grabbed a larger rock and pounded the crushed pile until the buds split and crumbled into the dirt. Out of breath, she stood and kicked dirt over it until it was unrecognizable from the rest of the granite pebbles that littered the dusty ground.

Anne reloaded her lunch box and snuck over to the orchard where half a dozen goats grazed on the weeds growing between the pear trees. Her grandpa and the ranch hands were far off, tilling the alfalfa fields. No one was around. Wind whistled around her, defeating the silent stillness.

Three rows away, she opened the lunchbox and tossed a small rock near to the goats, purposely missing them. They raised their heads and twitched their ears and flicked their tails and stared at her. She grabbed another rock and with unsteady boldness, threw another rock at the goat closest to her and hit it in the flank. The goat hopped and retreated further into the orchard. Anne narrowed her eyes, took a larger rock in her hands and steadily approached the goat, clustered with the others.

"Anne!" The voice in the wind came from behind her.

She spun around and there was her grandpa on horseback. He pulled the reins back to stop his chestnut brown mare, swung his leg over and hopped down.

Anne dropped the rocks in her hand and stood there speechless. Shame descended over her and tears streamed down her cheeks, warming the sting of the bitter cold.

Her grandpa said something to the horse, patted her rear, and strode over to Anne.

"Why are you doing that?" he chided, only feet from her. "Has that goat ever hurt you? Has she done anything to deserve you hurting her?"

Anne shook her head and cast her eyes down. "I'm sorry."

"I think the goat deserves your apology more than me, but I figure she's smart enough to keep her distance from you."

A tremor shot through Anne's body. She muttered "I'm sorry" again.

Her grandpa wrapped his arms around her and squeezed her in a tight hug. "I know you're mad at the world right now. I understand, but this is not the way to deal with it."

He squatted down and picked up a rock. "Look at this," he said, and turned the rock in his hands, sending the quartz shimmering in the sun. "Pretty ain't it?" He pointed to the horse then the goats. "Animals are like quartz."

Her chest heaved as she sobbed.

He lifted her chin. "Look at me, sweet pea. Everything has its place." He motioned towards a pile of leftover tumbleweeds waiting to be burned. "Except the tumbleweeds. You... me... the goats. Stop treating the animals like tumbleweeds. Let things be."

She blinked away the tears and wiped her face with her dirty sleeves.

He stood back up and dusted off his jeans. He took Anne's hand and led her back to the horse. "Mind helping me with Piper? She could use a brushing."

Inside the barn, Piper eyed Anne while she ran a brush across the mare's glossy coat. Her grandpa didn't say much as he hung up the saddle and blanket.

The horse whinnied.

Her grandpa nodded at Anne. "She wants a treat. Want to do the honors?"

Anne took the apple slices, slightly browned from the air, from his hand.

"Hold your palm open wide and she'll lick them right out of your hand," he said.

Anne did as instructed and raised her arm. Piper nuzzled her face close to the treat, tilted her head, and licked up the apples. Her tongue glided across Anne's skin, leaving a layer of saliva behind. Anne wiped her hands on her jeans.

Piper shook her head and her mane settled back down.

They locked eyes and a deep calm came over Anne. Kindness and forgiveness radiated from the beautiful creature's soul. Anne wished she had kindness and forgiveness in her own heart.

3

Dealing Differently

ALTHOUGH ANNE WAS BORN on April Fool's Day, her mom always told her she was never to be anyone's fool. She was determined to prove her mom right. It wasn't helping that everyone on the ranch referred to her as "Ms. Anne D.", a play on her name and her Grandpa Andy's name.

Anne poorly hid a scowl whenever Chuck, her grandpa's lead ranch hand, yelled out her moniker. Chuck's son Stevie, barely three years Anne's senior, was the only one on the ranch who refrained from calling her Ms. Anne D. Then again, she was pretty sure the boy was mute, because he hardly spoke more than a "g'morning" or "g'afternoon" to her. Stevie, tall and lanky in his jeans, boots, and cowboy hat, not only avoided talking to her, he avoided eye contact, too.

For Anne's twelfth birthday, Chuck's wife Marie said she would bake her a double layer German Chocolate cake, so

Anne made a mental note to let the whole Ms. Anne D. resentment go—at least for Chuck.

The guys broke for lunch when Marie showed up with the cake and little triangles of sandwiches on white bread—fancy like the tea parties from Anne's old life "down below." To locals, that phrase referred to anyone who lived south of the San Gabriel Mountains, below the 3,000-foot elevation of the High Desert.

Lovejoy was definitely no Beverly Hills. Still, Anne slipped her fork through the cake, ate the bite daintily and wiped her mouth as if she were back at home. She even convinced her grandpa to let them use the fine China that had belonged to her grandma with the promise that she herself would clean up afterward.

Marie stayed behind to help her while the guys returned to the duty of shearing the sheep. She pulled her hair back into a loose bun, which revealed the deep crows' lines around her brown eyes, then rolled up the sleeves on her blouse before getting to work on scrubbing dishes.

"I appreciate you helping," Anne said. She towel-dried the porcelain dishes and stacked them carefully. "The cake and sandwiches were delicious."

"You're most welcome, Ms. Anne D." Marie paused mid dish and glanced out the window. "It really is a shame about your parents. I knew your mom. Abby was the sweetest thing. Such a doll. Your dad Howie fell for her hard. Most guys in the area did." She resumed wiping the plate. Without making eye contact, she added, "You're pretty like your mom."

Anne's cheeks reddened. "Thank you." It was a kind thing to say, though, enamored by her mom's beauty, she felt it unfair to be compared to that high of a standard. Besides, she tried hard not to think of her parents—remembering wasn't going to bring them back.

"Not sure how busy you are helping out around here." Marie handed her the last dish. "You're welcome to come by my place. I could show you some needlepoint. You've seen those quilts of your grandma's, right? She taught me what she knew. I'd be happy to return the favor."

"Maybe I can do that sometime in the summer perhaps. I'm pretty busy with school." No, she wasn't. She hadn't had any homework that took her any time at all to do. She spent her afternoons reading books beside her window. And Anne never helped on the ranch. It wasn't something her grandpa expected of her. Why should she get her hands dirty when her grandpa had Chuck, his son Stevie, and other guys when needed to help? She'd only get in the way.

Marie wiped her hands on her apron. She crossed the room to return the stack of dishes to the China cabinet and paused. "When's the last time this place was dusted? My goodness." She set down the plates. "Why don't you grab a rag and give me a hand here?"

Anne wasn't used to dusting or doing more than straightening up. Back home, they had a housekeeper who came in once a week to do that sort of thing. Things were different out here. She helped Marie rub the shelves off before returning the plates to their spots, no longer on circles surrounded by dust.

Maria gently pressed the glass doors shut. "To be honest with you, dusting is a never-ending job around here. Doesn't matter how often you do it. Dirt still finds a way in."

"So why bother?" Anne's eyes widened. She hadn't realized she'd said this aloud.

Marie threw back her head and laughed. "Guess that should be the motto, right? Why bother?"

By the summer, with the weather scorching, Anne woke up earlier and earlier. With a hatred of mornings, she wasn't happy with the sun streaming through the curtains in her bedroom and warming her face.

One morning she awoke to darkness. Unsure of the time, she glanced out the window. A dim glow appeared on the distant horizon. She groaned and lay back in bed with her eyes wide open, staring up into nothing. The front door swung open and shut. Her grandpa's footsteps on the hard-packed dirt passed beyond her window, likely headed to the barn. Sure enough, the dogs whined at his approach. What was he doing? Getting Piper ready? Feeding the chickens? Letting out the goats?

Did he always wake up so early? She pulled the pillow over her head. Sleep. Sleep. Sleep. If she said it enough times, maybe her brain would comply.

Not this time. She peered out the curtain. A faint gray sliver of light glowed in the east. With resignation, she sat up and pulled on shorts and a T-shirt. She slipped on her sneakers and strode outside as day rapidly gained headway over the night.

The cool air blew against her bare skin giving her goosebumps. When she drew closer to the barn, she paused. A faint whimper in the distance caught her attention. She did a 360. Nothing out of the ordinary. No coyote howls, although they could be sneaky. Crickets chirped. Something scampered away in the nearby creosote bushes.

At the barn, she peered in through the cracked open doors, squinting into the darkness. On a bench next to Piper, her grandpa sat hunched over. Every few moments, his shoulders shook. One of the cattle dogs lay beside him.

She approached with caution. The dog raised his head and tracked her location with ears on alert. Another sniffle and her grandpa's shoulders shook.

Anne's throat tightened. Had she made him mad? To view a big, tough guy in such a vulnerable position, she felt as if she shouldn't be there. She'd invaded his space and privacy. Maybe she could sneak back out. The dog rose to its feet alerting her grandpa who turned to face her. He wiped his eyes with his shirt sleeve.

"Anne?" he asked, his voice small. "Is that you?"

"Grandpa?" Her feet were planted in place. "Sorry, I didn't mean to disturb—I'll go."

He shook his head and patted the other end of the bench. "You're not disturbing me. Come have a seat."

She did as she was told but avoided looking into his tear-streaked face. This somehow must be her fault. She hadn't been the easiest to deal with. "Did I make you sad?" she asked. "I'm sorry. I can help you out more. I don't want you to cry."

He let out a heavy sigh. "It's not your fault. Grief is a part of life. We all deal with it in different ways." He held up his fists in a mock fist fight then pointed at her. "You're angry." He pointed at himself. "Me? I'm sad. Both are normal parts of grieving."

"Why are you sad?"

"She was your mom, but she was my little girl. Parents aren't supposed to bury their children. That makes three out of six of mine gone."

Anne cast her eyes down, ashamed that she hadn't understood that anyone beyond herself could be sad. Would the polite thing be to ask him which six he was referring to, or to say nothing in hopes that the uncomfortable moment would pass?

As if reading her mind, he continued, "Yes, six. Your grandma Alice, the most beautiful, lovely woman that ever walked this earth, died when the sixth was born back in 1932. Horrible losing both Alice and the baby." His chest heaved with a sob. "We had two boys, Eddie and Mikey. Then the baby girl. That was the first one we lost—poor sweet little Doris died from the flu before she turned a month old. That was rough on all of us, our first little girl."

Anne didn't know much about her aunts and uncles. This was the first she'd ever heard of Doris. She sat and listened and tried hard not to feel anything at all.

"Bobby was a good boy and then came your mom. Alice and I adored baby Abby." Another heavy sigh. "She was supposed to be the last baby. Wish we could turn back time on getting pregnant again. James was the death of her. Oh, God, yes, he was." More tears. Another wipe of the sleeve. "Only glad Alice wasn't around when the oldest two went off to the war. She never had to live through losing Eddie on D-Day. Well, we lost Mikey, too, even though he came back alive, shell-shocked." He gave Anne a sympathetic smile. "Your mom. She was the one who stuck around and helped me and Bobby and cheered us up when we got sad about the whole thing. She had the sparkle of Alice in her through and through."

Her grandpa wrapped an arm around her shoulders and squeezed her. "You have that same spark."

Deaf to the compliment, Anne bit her lip to keep from crying. Not only had she lost her parents, but she was incredibly selfish. Her grandpa probably hated her.

"Hey," he said. "Growing up is learning how to live in the bodies we're given and deal with the emotions that come with all that. Trust me, it's better to let it out than to hold it all in."

The chickens clucked from the other end of the barn.

He stood up, twisted, and cracked his back. "That's better. You can head back to bed if you'd like. I've got to feed the chickens and collect the eggs."

Anne stood and pulled herself up straight. "I can help."

"Yes." He smiled. "Yes, you sure can."

4

The Ranch

For the rest of the summer, Anne settled into a routine: wake up at dawn, fetch the eggs from the chickens, refill their food and water and that of the dogs while her grandpa tended to the goats, sheep, and horses until Chuck and Stevie arrived to help.

By mid-morning, the blazing sun beat down on them. Animals and people took refuge in the shade, with the dogs lapping up water. Speech got slower with more pauses between words. Chuck and her grandpa wandered down the rows of pears, remaining in the safety of their shade.

Anne settled down under the limited shade of a large Joshua Tree and drew squiggles and shapes with a stick in the loose top layer of sediment. The blue sky was clear of birds with the occasional crack of a jet overhead breaking the sound barrier—something she'd never witnessed down below. Her grandpa often bragged about the famous Chuck Yeager who was first to fly faster than the speed of sound in a Bell X-1 plane. He had taken off from Edwards Air Force Base in October of 1947—"While you were still a baby in britches."

When harvest time came around, activity on the ranch increased with half a dozen temporary workers showing up daily to help with the alfalfa and pears.

"With seventy acres of alfalfa, one cutting takes us at least a week," her grandpa explained.

"Cutting?" Anne imagined a long pair of shears trimming the crops.

"Mowing, raking, and baling." He wiped his brow and fanned his face with his hat.

"Raking?" That would take way more time than scooping up the crunchy leaves on the lawn under the sycamore trees back home.

Her grandpa laughed. "Why don't you saddle up and come watch? Got to keep a distance though. The horses can get spooked by the tractor. It wasn't long ago that they were pulling the machines."

Intrigued, she followed her grandpa who helped her mount Duke, a gelding, one of the half dozen Quarter Horses on the ranch. Anne knew Piper and Comet—a strong gelding who was Chuck's favorite—and Sienna, an older mare ridden by Stevie, as well as Gunner, a sometimes helpful but problematic stallion that was kept separate from the others. A bit fearful of the way Gunner stared her down, Anne avoided him. She gained the trust of the others, aided by treating them with carrots and apples whenever her grandpa let her.

She rode out after her grandpa who hitched Piper to a fence post near the crops where the horse could rest and drink water from the trough.

"I've already mowed with the tractor-drawn sickle-bar," he said. "Gave the alfalfa a few days to dry out—doesn't take much in this heat. Today, we're raking to get it ready for the baling machine."

"It's so hot," she said. "Can't you wait until it cools off?"

"Leave it too long and it gets brittle and loses its nutrient levels. You can hang out here until I take a break."

From there, her grandpa strode out to the tractor. It came to life with the growl of the engine. Piper wasn't bothered. Her coat glistened in the sun.

Even with a hat on, Anne was overcome with the heat. Sweat accumulated under her shirt—Grandpa made her wear a long-sleeved one to avoid a nasty sunburn. Her jeans clung to her sticky legs, and her feet were damp in her new boots. She took a swig of water from the canteen across her chest, yet dizziness settled in.

How could her grandpa enjoy this life? Define misery and this was it.

"You hot, too, Duke?" Anne whispered to her horse. He turned his ears and moved his head around. "I'll take that as a yes."

Waving at her grandpa who pulled a wide rake behind the tractor in the opposite direction, she spurred Duke towards him. Her grandpa was near the end of his property line.

She dug her heels into Duke's side to goad him forward across the field. The closer they got to the tractor, the more the horse resisted. The poor thing.

Her grandpa turned the tractor and headed in her direction.

Duke neighed and shook the reins, refusing to go forward. He was clearly exhausted.

Anne waved her arms rapidly at her grandpa.

Duke paced and pawed at the ground, breathing heavily through his nostrils. Anne pictured him falling to the ground.

Her grandpa took off his hat and waved it at her aggressively. What was he trying to say?

Anne tried to urge Duke forward. Normally docile, he wasn't listening to her commands. She shook the reins and kicked his sides. "Come on, Duke, what's wrong with you?"

Her grandpa killed the engine to the tractor and marched towards her, yelling.

When he was finally in earshot, she could make out what he was saying.

"What in God's name are you doing?" he screamed. "Trying to get yourself killed?"

Anne held tight to the reins to keep Duke in place. "What do you mean? It's hot out here. I want to go back."

"Who's stopping you from heading back? Can't you tell he's spooked? Use your head before he kicks you off."

She realized she'd misread Duke's stubbornness for heat stroke. Her cheeks reddened. "I thought he—I didn't know. Sorry, grandpa."

"Duke's the one you need to be apologizing to." He shook his head. "Luckily, he has enough sense not to throw you off. Go back and have Chuck help you with Duke."

"Where is he?"

"In the orchards picking the pears. Where you should be, too. Leave the crops to me."

As soon as she turned Duke in the opposite direction, he became much more responsive to her commands, with only an occasional shudder running through his body. Embarrassed at her ignorance, Anne cursed the ranch and the desert and even her grandpa the whole way around the buttes.

"How is this my damn fault?" She grumbled. "He's the one who dragged me out to the fields. Now somehow, I'm the one who messed up? I wish I wasn't even here."

The pear orchards grew closer. Chuck, Stevie, and a half-dozen other men were in varying stages of picking. The few on ladders handed off small baskets of the pears to others on the ground who carefully packed them in cases.

"Chuck," she called out.

He descended a ladder and wiped his hands on his jeans. "What is it, Ms. Anne D.?"

"Grandpa asked if you could help me put away Duke."

Chuck looked puzzled so she mumbled an explanation as he gave her the side-eye.

"Damn near killed yourself." He shook his head. "I'm in the middle of this right now. These pears aren't going to pick themselves and we can't let them get soft." He turned and whistled. "Hey, Stevie, get over here."

Stevie set down his basket and strode their way.

On his way into tenth grade, Stevie was taller than Anne had realized, almost as tall as Chuck—a better-looking, baby-faced version of his father, with thicker hair and reddened skin.

True to his typical behavior, Stevie didn't say much. Instead, he helped Anne down and grabbed the reins to walk Duke back to the barn. She walked on Stevie's far side, unsure of whether Duke would kick her out of anger.

In the stall, Stevie took off the saddle and hung it up. "Whaddya do?"

"Oh, Stevie speaks?" She rolled her eyes.

"Can you stop calling me that?" He pulled off the blankets and hung them up.

She blinked and scrunched up her face. "Calling you what?"

"Stevie," he said. "My name is Stephen. Maybe Steve. But not Stevie."

"That's what everyone—"

"What's that, Ms. Anne D.?"

She scowled. "I hate that name."

"I know the feeling."

She blushed. Why hadn't he said anything before? Then again, neither had she.

"Okay, *Steve*," she emphasized his name. "That better?"

"Much better, *Anne*. Mind giving me a hand?"

"Doing what?"

"Why don't you refill his water?" He snorted. "Do you help your grandpa at all?"

She stomped over to the spigot and dragged the hose over. "As a matter of fact, I do. I collect eggs every morning. I feed the chickens and give the animals water."

"That's not a bad start." He raised an eyebrow. "For a little girl."

Anne huffed and narrowed her eyes at him. She was almost thirteen and going into seventh grade, hardly a *little girl*. She reminded herself not to say anything that would get her in trouble with her grandpa who was already irritated enough with her. Instead, she gave *Steve* the silent treatment for the rest of the time until they had finished up.

"Time for me to get back and pick some more pears," he said. "They won't pick themselves." With that, he turned and marched back in the direction they'd come.

She turned to Duke. "He can go die in a ditch," she said. "It is hot out after all."

Duke swung his head and avoided eye contact.

"Fine, you're mad at me, too. Everyone's mad at me. Anne can't do anything right. Well, I don't care." With that, she went inside to take a shower, prepare lunch, and read a book.

She snuggled up on the corner of her bed and opened her novel, *The Lion, the Witch, and the Wardrobe*.

"Where's my magic wardrobe?" she asked aloud. "Wish I could get the hell out of here."

A sliver of blinding sunlight struck her in the face through the gap in the curtains.

She grumbled and turned towards the wall.

5

Sienna

In school, Anne turned the other way when mothers showed up to assist the teacher—that was no concern of hers.

Besides, she had to save her energy to help her grandpa however she could on the ranch, be it brushing patterns into the horses' coats, playing fetch with the dogs, or chasing the goats between the pear trees—none of which constituted help in the traditional sense but all of which brought a smile to her grandpa's face, something Anne increasingly focused on doing.

Steve was in high school and got home later than her on account of the bus ride, so he only came over to the ranch on the weekends, which was fine by her.

On one Saturday morning, she taunted Steve by tossing rocks at his feet while he was on a ladder pruning a pear tree.

"Would you quit it already?" Steve yelled at her as he descended the rungs.

"Quit what?" She leaned against the trunk of a tree with her hands behind her back, one palm gripping another rock.

"You're so immature," he said. "Why don't *you* try pruning a tree?"

"I'm just a little girl," she said, as she kicked at the dirt with the toe of her shoe. "How could I lift a big heavy pole saw?"

"I have a lopper for you." He motioned to a tool on the ground. "I'm sure your tiny little girl hands can pick that one up."

"I wouldn't want to mess it up and trim the wrong branch."

"Don't you have someone else you can bother?" He smirked. "Why don't you take Duke or one of the other horses out to watch your grandpa run the tractor on the alfalfa fields?"

Someone cursing in the distance made both of them turn their heads in that direction.

"God damn it!" Chuck came galloping up on Comet. He pulled the reins back and came to a sudden halt, kicking up a cloud of dust. "Where's your grandpa?" he yelled at Anne.

She pointed to the end of Lovejoy Buttes. "Out in the fields."

Chuck shook his head. "Stevie, get back to the barn and help me secure Gunner."

"What happened?" Steve asked.

"He's decided to engage in some pasture breeding with Sienna." Chuck kicked his heels at Comet's sides, and they took off again, coating Anne and Steve in a wall of dirt.

Steve trotted after his father and Anne followed, asking "What happened to Sienna?"

"You've got to be kidding," he said. "What part of breeding do you not understand?"

When Chuck and Steve tried to separate the two horses, Gunner charged at them and kicked. He returned to Sienna and, when she sidled away from him, he bit her. Sienna ran toward the barn and the stallion followed close behind.

Anne kept a distance while the men secured Gunner back into his separate corral. Gunner neighed, grunted, and pawed at the ground.

"How did he get out?" Her grandpa wiped his brow with the bandana hanging around his neck. "He was locked up when I left this morning."

Each of them glanced around, but no one fessed up to it.

"Where there's a will, there's a way," Chuck said. He threw up his hands. "Isn't she a little old to breed?"

"How will we know if she's pregnant?" Steve asked.

Anne's grandpa shrugged. "Eventually, we'll figure it out, I 'spose. In a year, there'll either be another horse or there won't be."

Sienna neighed and flicked her tail at them.

Six months later, in spring of 1961, it became apparent that Sienna wasn't bloated but was in fact pregnant. Anne spent her afternoons—when it wasn't blistering cold or burning hot—sitting on the boulders at the edge of the buttes, reading books and observing Sienna for signs of movement in her belly.

"You're wasting your time," her grandpa said when he strolled by. "Nothing interesting is going to happen until late August or early September."

"Maybe it's not interesting to you," she said. "To me it is."

A gust of wind flipped the pages of her book and whipped her hair into her face.

She pulled the hair from her mouth and spit out the dirt. A stronger gust blew the book right out of her lap. It landed face down on the ground.

"I hate the wind," she said. "It's awful. Either it's cold and windy or hot and windy but it's always too windy."

"Would you rather the heat beat down on your skin without the relief of a breeze?"

"Breeze?" She rolled her eyes. That term was reserved for the waves of air that gently tossed the flowers in the garden back home—meaning that place that was no longer home.

Anne marched over to pick up her book. A strong breeze caught her and pushed her back a step. She lost her balance, tripped over a rock, and tumbled down.

Her grandpa held out his hand to help her up. "Learn to sway with the wind. Stop fighting it. The wind will win every time."

"I'm not trying to fight it. It's picking on me." She brushed off her jeans.

"The wind ain't got any feelings about you, or anything else." He motioned at the buttes, the desert fields and the sky. "You can't control the wind, and you can't control the sun. The best you can do is to prepare for both or risk being destroyed by them." With that, he pulled his bandana up over his mouth and nose. "Whenever things go wrong on the ranch, which is often, I repeat that saying. Saves me quite a bit of cursing and headaches."

By August, Sienna's belly had grown considerably, and there were lumps and bumps that poked out. Anne's grandpa said the foal would eventually get tired of being cramped up in there and decide to make its appearance. Each new day before she collected the eggs and fed the animals, Anne checked if there was a baby horse in the stall with Sienna. There wasn't.

"The AV Fair's coming up," her grandpa said one morning while he was saddling up Piper. "Would you like to come help out this year?"

Anne's eyes widened. "Definitely. What do I get to do?"

"We've got a couple of sheep and a goat up for a possible ribbon. You can help with them. Or…" He gave a dramatic pause. "You can take care of the baby chick display."

She squealed. Cute, fluffy chicks were the most adorable things on the ranch—not right after they hatched when they were all sticky and sweaty and exhausted, but when they were fluffed out like tiny stuffed animals. The fuzzy balls peeped and pecked and in general were some of the cutest things, next to puppies and kittens.

"You and Steve can take care of the exhibit and answer questions about them."

"Steve?" She didn't hide her disappointment.

"Well, sure, he's been doing this since he was your age."

Three years didn't exactly make him an expert in her mind.

Early on the first day, while it was still more dark than light, her grandpa had her and Steve help lead the animals up a ramp and into the wood-slotted pens built into the bed of his old Chevy pickup truck. The sheep baa'd and the goat bleated at them while the latches on their temporary enclosures were secured in place. They'd be displayed in the corrals at the fair.

The chick display had a lot of moving parts to load, including heat lamps and glass cases and, of course, delicate eggs waiting to hatch. Every time they hit a bump in the road,

Anne's stomach dipped like she was on a roller coaster and she stared back at the precious cargo.

Anne hadn't been in the cab of the truck much, except to get bales of hay or groceries up in town, and this was her first time nestled between her grandpa and sixteen-year-old Steve, who sat with an elbow out the window. The wind whipped the few loose strands of her hair around and she was glad to have tightly braided it the night before while it was still wet from her bath.

They drove north on the recently paved 170th Street East and headed west on the straight two-lane Avenue O towards Lancaster, all before dawn broke.

"Next year," her grandpa said, his words half lost in the wind, "when you start high school, you'll take a bus up this way to AV High."

She nodded, picturing a bigger school with bigger people—a bunch of female versions of Steve all towering over her, teasing and mocking her. She shuddered and focused on the asphalt in front of them.

The truck hit a pothole. She braced herself against the dash to keep from hitting her head against the back window. Her muscles tensed.

It was a surprise to find herself more uncomfortable in the truck cab than on the back of a horse. Her life had become so different in the two years since her parents passed. From peaceful tree-lined streets and mansions—she knew by now that's how others referred to the big houses—to the bleak desert landscape of tumbleweeds and Joshua Trees.

The area had grown on her. At least she didn't hate it as much as she did. Maybe familiarity breeds comfort, which could be mistaken for fondness.

After they unloaded the sheep and goat at the fairground's corrals, they got to work assisting other local farmers and ranchers with the indoor chick display. Half the enclosure was set aside for eggs about to hatch, where pecking beaks would soon emerge from the inside of shells, the other half was for fluffy chicks already toddling around in the straw.

"The biggest hassle you'll deal with here," her grandpa said, "is that everyone wants to take a chick home with them."

"Are we giving them away?" she asked, as a protective urge overcame her. Maybe she didn't want to let strangers around the chicks.

"Absolutely not," her grandpa said. "Animals are a responsibility." Another rancher tapped him on the shoulder and pulled him away for some matter that needed attending to.

"Chicks aren't souvenirs," Steve said. He leaned against the wall, his boots polished, and his belt buckle shined. Indoors without his cowboy hat, he was a stranger to her. Curls of his brown hair rested on his forehead and covered the nape of his neck.

"So why bring everything up here if we aren't selling them?" she asked.

Steve laughed. Was it in jest? Had she said something funny?

"I'm serious," she said. "What's with all the trouble of setting this up?"

"Not everyone who comes to the fair lives on a ranch or farm. There are a lot of kids who have never seen a chicken hatch."

"Oh." She turned away and focused on a tiny beak breaking through a crack in its shell.

My, her life had indeed changed. What was commonplace now would've been an incredible wonder to behold not too long ago.

At the end of the day, they left the chick display there. Her grandpa promised her the bigger chicks wouldn't peck the newest ones to death overnight—although Anne didn't quite believe him.

Hot and sweaty and covered in a layer of grime, she was glad to have the windows open while they headed back home.

Her grandpa slowed down when they crossed under the gateway. He pulled the truck up behind the house. No sooner had he killed the engine than Chuck was there waving at them.

"Come on. She's here!" Chuck exclaimed.

The three of them stared at him, perplexed.

"Who?" her grandpa asked.

"It's a girl." Chuck grinned and gestured for them to follow him to the barn.

"We missed it?" Anne hurried ahead. "I can't believe we missed it. You said Sienna wasn't going to have her baby yet."

"Not like you can plan these things," her grandpa said. "Babies come when they're good and ready to."

Sure enough, inside the barn, Sienna was no longer alone in her pen.

"How'd that happen?" Anne gaped at the size of the foal.

"Did someone explain the birds and bees to her?" Steve shook his head.

She blushed. "I know that. I meant how did something that big come out of her?"

"The usual way," Chuck told her, as he watched her grandpa checking out the foal. "Four legs, two ears, and a tail," he said, adding, "Don't worry. She passed the 1-2-3." He turned to Anne and explained. "Stood within one hour, nursed within two, afterbirth passed within three."

Anne stared at the wobbly newborn. That was too many details for her liking.

Her grandpa grinned. "Now we got to name her."

"Trixie?" Chuck said.

"More like a Rosie," her grandpa said. "Her coloring is like Sienna's."

Anne peered over the wooden rail. "Sage."

They threw her curious looks.

"Pretty, like desert sage," she said. "And grows wild."

"I sure hope you're wrong on that one." Her grandpa said. "The last thing we need around here is a wild horse." He turned to the foal. "What do you think? Like the name Sage?"

The baby shook its mane and nudged Sienna.

His grandpa nodded. "All right. Sage it is."

6

Times Have Changed

WITH A STUBBORN STREAK of independence, Sage grew into her name. Anne grew out of hers.

In an outburst prefaced by "with all due respect," Steve informed his dad, her grandpa, and the other ranch hands that he was no longer to be referred to as Stevie. "And Anne is ready to start high school, so I figure you all should stop calling her Ms. Anne D. Just Anne will do."

Contrary to her expectations, this announcement was met with a shrug of indifference. From that point on, he was Steve and she was Anne and nobody acted as if it had ever been any different. Grateful, she called a truce while they trimmed pear trees side-by-side.

"I'll quit being a pain in the ass to you," she said. "As a token of thanks."

"So incredibly generous of you," Steve said. "Perhaps because it's unbecoming of a young lady turning fourteen to tease the hired help."

She tossed a late-harvest pear at him, which he caught. "Since when did you start using all of those fancy words?"

He shrugged and took a bite of the pear, wiping away the juices that ran down his chin. With his mouth full, he said, "It's an upperclassmen thing you wouldn't understand."

"Okay, so now you get to tease me?" She shook her head and trimmed off a branch that tumbled to the ground and landed atop the hard dirt with a bounce.

"I've got my driver's license. That makes me more mature." He smirked and tossed down the stem of the finished fruit.

How could she take him seriously? He had a cowlick sticking up in the back of his head and a swirl of pear juice on his T-shirt.

Over a hearty meal of stew with meat, potatoes, and carrots, Anne broached the subject of high school with her grandpa, telling him she was nervous.

"Hate to admit it," her grandpa said, "but I didn't make it past ninth grade."

She widened her eyes. "Is that true? You're so smart, I would've never guessed."

"A formal education doesn't make you smart. Not being formally educated doesn't make you dumb. It's the other choices you make in life. I've always read a lot."

She glanced over at the dusty bookcase in the corner. Its contents were stacked double wide and more books were layered atop. The shelves were dusty, so she hadn't given any thought as to why the bookcase was still there.

"Why'd you stop?" she asked.

"Reading or school? Reading because I ran out of books and the little library out here couldn't keep up with me. School for a number of reasons."

"Like?" She finished the last of her stew, wiped her mouth, and stared at him.

"My parents wanted me to quit. Hell, I wanted me to. That road to town wasn't paved until 1930. Before that, we traveled by horse and buggy on dirt roads with other kids from local homesteads. Twenty-six miles is an unbearable amount of time by buggy, up to five hours each way. On horseback it's two and a half hours if you really push it."

"No cars?"

"Not many."

Anne had never realized how privileged she was to be living in a modern time of paved roads and cars and buses.

"How could anyone go to school?"

"Some of the kids boarded up there with the schoolteacher during the week." He paused. "Course that's not practical when you're helping out on the ranch."

"Will the bus ride take two hours?" The grim possibility sank her heart.

Her grandpa placed a reassuring hand on hers. "Don't you mind. It won't. And you're going to finish high school. No doubt about that. Your mom did. Your uncles did. You will."

Secretly she wondered if Steve would drive to high school his senior year, and if so, would he let a lowly freshman tag along? Having heard that he was going steady with a girl from school, she gave up on any wishful thinking. And another thing—it irked her to overhear him talking about *that girl* to the other guys working the ranch. Why should anyone care?

That summer, she mentally prepared herself to move up to the big high school. She'd be forced to be friendly with other girls. The tea parties with her friends down below were no more than a fuzzy memory, a made-up scene in a book.

Out here, she favored solitude. Once her chores were over, she studied the hawks that soared in the wind, the rabbits that scurried in the fields, the quails that sprinted from one creosote bush to the next, and even the steady presence of the Joshua trees. In the afternoons, she had grown fond of taking Duke out to the spring and hiking alongside the rocky buttes.

One evening, after telling her grandpa where she'd be, she hiked up to the top of Lovejoy Buttes to view the sunset. Her grandpa insisted on her waiting for a full moon and bringing a flashlight and made her promise "not to kill yourself getting down."

The quiet evening brought her peace, and made the trip worthwhile, though the loose rocks made her stumble and slip a few feet down a couple of times during her descent. She wouldn't mention that to him and risk losing her independence.

Late summer was roasting hot. Her grandpa said it was the same every year but that she had selective memory and was choosing to forget.

As time went by, she offered more assistance, including cleaning the horse stalls.

Bringing the heavy bales of hay and alfalfa to the barn to feed the horses was still too hard for her. Whenever he was around, Steve took care of it.

Anne refilled the troughs with water and gazed at Steve out of the corner of her eye while he toiled around the barn. Even on hot days, outside he wore long sleeves, jeans, and his cowboy hat to protect himself from the sun. In the barn though, he got down to a T-shirt which showcased his biceps and triceps, as pronounced as his wide shoulders.

She turned back to tend to the chickens lest he think she was staring.

Sage turned out to be a handful as she grew. Anne tried not to take on the guilt for naming her, knowing the name alone wasn't responsible for her skittishness or reluctance to engage with humans. She was also spooked by sheep, goats, dogs and sudden movements.

"If she's going to be a useful ranch horse, her personality has to change," her grandpa said.

Anne scrunched her forehead. "What do you mean by that?"

"Chuck and I think she's got some issues and isn't developing as a filly should."

"What's going to happen to her?"

"We'll wait it out another couple of years. If we don't observe a noticeable improvement in her temperament by then, it may come time to say our goodbyes."

She glanced over at Sage, in the stall by herself next to Sienna. "What do you mean?"

"We weaned her later than normal to help her, but we've got Sienna's health to consider."

"Are you going to kill her?"

Her grandpa shook his head. "When have you known me to kill a perfectly good animal? We'd sell her off to someone else who has the time and energy to train her."

Anne stared into Sage's eyes. Sage stared back.

"I can train her."

"You don't know the first thing about training a horse. You can barely ride one."

Her cheeks reddened. "I can, too."

"Walking and trotting, yes. Galloping, should Sage choose to do that while you're on her back—no. Not going to risk you getting hurt. I didn't say we'd give up on her yet. We'll try saddle training her in another year. She can't support the weight of a rider until she's three or four. To be honest, that's a long time to have another mouth to feed."

Her grandpa wiped off his hands on a rag and headed out back to check on the crops. He had a slight limp in his gait and wasn't as spry as he was a few years earlier. "Pushing sixty" as he referred to himself had brought gradual changes in his energy and more aches and pains. Anne would pretend not to notice until he admitted it, which was highly unlikely.

Her other grandparents, her dad's mom and dad, had to be in their late seventies by now. She hadn't visited them since before her parents died. The best she got was a birthday card and another card on Christmas with a check for five dollars with the word "gift" written on the memo line.

Her grandpa made her handwrite a thank you note each time. She didn't mind, but didn't see the point in it. Money was a poor replacement for a fractured relationship. When her dad died—their only child—apparently so too had their love. Maybe Anne wasn't worthy of their love. They had, after all, refused to take her in.

There was no other valid excuse in her opinion, which, as instructed by her grandpa, she kept to herself. He'd often warn her that "Opinions are like asses. Everyone's got one and everybody thinks everyone else's stinks."

Sage tucked her tail and trembled, nostrils flared and eyes wide, whenever anyone approached. Anyone except Anne.

In the morning after collecting eggs, she pulled up a stool in front of Sage and sat with apple slices in her hand. Anne didn't say anything, simply stared into the filly's eyes.

Eventually, Sage approached and sniffed the air.

Anne held out her open palm with a couple of the smaller slices.

Sage backed away then approached once more. She reached out her neck, lapped up the apples, and retreated.

"Listen up, Sage." Anne peered between the wood slats. "I promise I won't let them take you away. I know you have value, even if no one else does. You need to believe it, too, and learn to trust people. Not everyone is out to hurt you."

Sage shook her mane and flicked her tail.

Maybe Anne needed to believe that of herself as well.

7

Rough Patch

Anne savored the last bite of her ham and cheese sandwich and reached for a pear. Wind whistled as loud as a train engine, blasting the side of the house with dirt. She jumped up and pushed aside the curtains. Waves of dirt rushed by, airborne. The window rattled with each blast of dust. Lovejoy Buttes, normally a beautiful backdrop out the dining room window, had disappeared. The window shook and granules of dust collected in the sill. The screen door banged open and shut.

They'd had a few of these dust storms before, which could last for hours. Travel was impossible because roads, paved or not, were impassable. She peered into the distance. In between the oscillations of dusty wind, her grandpa's truck was visible. The entire front end was consumed by dry tumbleweeds, larger than she. A gust picked up a few and blew them to the side. More piled up in a mound as tall as the truck.

Her stomach sank. Her grandpa, Chuck and Steve, the animals—all caught in the desert storm. Part of her wished to stay in her room and hide under a blanket. Why sacrifice her safety?

The men were no doubt securing the horses and sheep—that's usually the way these things went. What about the poor goats? She shook her head, and, despite it being hot and dry, put on one of her coats and tied a scarf around her face. She reached for her new sunglasses then stopped. What good would they be in the wind with dirt sliding through the sides and top and bottom. The lenses would get scratched up, in addition to her eyes getting dust in them.

Downstairs, she opened the front door and the heavy wooden door flew open. With much effort, she secured it shut and headed into the wall of dirt in the direction of the orchard where the goats had been munching on weeds earlier in the day.

Leaning into the wind at an angle with her head down, she fought against the gusts. For each three steps forward, she got pushed back one. Her hair whipped sharply in her face and stung her bare skin. The scarf unraveled and she shoved it into a pocket.

This was worse than usual. Where was everyone?

"Grandpa?" she called out. "Steve? Chuck?"

Nothing responded but the wind.

A momentary break in the dirt revealed a wave of tumbleweeds headed straight for her.

Heart racing, she sprinted out of the way. More kept coming. She ran further. They rolled by her propelled forward by the wind.

Where were the pear trees? She should've reached them already.

Another gust sent handfuls of dirt against her. She kept her head turned away and squeezed her eyes shut. Even with her lips pursed, dirt had weaseled its way in. She spat out the dirt and spun around trying to get her bearings. The sun and sky were engulfed in dirt, and the air glowed an eerie orange.

"Grandpa!" she yelled.

Where was she? Her visibility had shrunk to a few feet in front of her outstretched arms. Dirt pelted her jeans. She scanned her surroundings. No pear trees. No house or truck. No barn or buttes. More tumbleweeds rolled by.

Panic overcame her. "Grandpa!" she screamed louder.

In the distance, the dogs barked.

A momentary reprieve in the wind dropped the dirt back to the ground. In front of her was a split rail fence. Somehow, she had wandered to the edge of the property and nearly made her way through the gateway into the desert fields.

Forget about the pear trees and the goats. She jogged up the gravel road back toward the house. Loose sediment swirled into a funnel in front of her, catching weeds and debris in its grip. The dust devil passed over and around her. She covered her face with her hands and waited. The breeze died down and dust settled back to the desert floor.

She reached the house. The side was covered to the bottom of the eaves with a tightly packed wall of tumbleweeds.

They'd have to wait for the next burn day, whenever the wind subsided, pile them up and burn them. With the wind calmed for a few minutes—as unpredictable as it was, it could pick back up in a moment—she hurried further to the barn.

Her grandpa, Chuck, and Steve were corralling the last of the animals into the barn.

"Where were you?" her grandpa asked. "I went by the house to get you to help, and you had clean disappeared."

"The wind and dirt...I couldn't see a thing near the pear trees," she said. "I was searching for the goats."

"In the wrong direction." Steve wiped his face with his sleeve.

"We got them when the winds picked up, earlier," her grandpa said, leaning against a post to catch his breath. "We got the dogs to help us." His chest heaved as inhaled and exhaled. "Going to sit down for a bit." He settled onto the bench and leaned back against the wall.

"Damn winds." Chuck secured the back doors shut. "Last thing we need when it's hotter than hell." He glanced at her grandpa, threw Steve a look, and shook his head.

Steve announced on the last day of summer that he'd be riding the bus to school the same as Anne. After all, gas was thirty-three cents a gallon and "money didn't grow on trees." He tried to get a part-time job in Palmdale. With minimum wage at $1.25 an hour and Chuck's truck getting twelve miles per gallon at best, the fifty-mile roundtrip to town hardly made getting a job worth it. He said he wasn't going to go through all that trouble to work two hours of a shift just for the privilege of making more than the piecemeal money from the ranch work.

Anne got ready for school and slipped into her new dress and saddle shoes—clothes she bought with the money she'd saved up from her other grandparents' checks.

She stepped up onto the bus and glanced around for a familiar face. There were two girls from Wilsona School that she recognized. They were friends with each other, not her, as they made perfectly clear by ignoring her as she made her way down the aisle. Where was Steve? The seats were high and anyone who slouched became invisible behind the vinyl boundaries. Though it was not as if a senior would deign to hold a seat for a freshman. Who was she kidding?

The driver told her to take a seat, so Anne slid into an empty seat midway back and stared out the window. It was still half-dark, a time of day she was used to from working on the ranch.

The ride was bumpier than in her grandpa's Chevy.

As the sun crept over the horizon, the silhouettes of Joshua Trees took shape in the distance. By the time they neared Lancaster, it was hot and sunny. The school buildings were bigger than anything out in Lovejoy or the neighboring Wilsona Gardens.

Anne inhaled a deep breath, slung her backpack over her shoulder and exited the bus. Was she on a college campus? The girls and boys that moseyed about seemed twice her size. She was a little girl placed in the wrong school, an outsider who didn't belong.

After sorting out where she was supposed to be and when—she had to change classrooms for the first time—she found a vacant space under a shady tree. No tumbleweeds or Joshua Trees on campus. Thank goodness.

A group of three girls with fully developed boobs approached in sophisticated pencil skirts that barely covered their knees and high ponytails tied with scarves—definitely upperclassmen. Anne shrunk into herself and hugged her knees.

A tall blonde girl stepped forward. "Hi. You must be new. I'm Linda. This is Nancy and Mary. What's your name?"

Anne blushed and introduced herself.

"Nice to meet you, Anne," Linda said. "This spot is ours. So, if you wouldn't mind, we'd like it back."

Anne tripped over herself getting to her feet. She apologized and hurried off.

From behind her, Linda said loudly, "What kind of country hick did the cat drag in?" The other girls laughed.

Anne bit her lower lip to keep from crying. She found the girls' restroom and hid in a stall while other giggling girls busied themselves applying lipstick in front of the mirrors. After they left, Anne hurried out and stood in front of the mirror. Her dress was old-fashioned.

She sighed and took her hair out of its braid. It fell forward and hid her face.

The teachers were nice enough and the other kids mostly ignored her, so Anne sought comfort in the school library, which became her hangout. At least she could check out new books to read. She didn't need to hang out in the heat with gossiping girls, she could relax in the air-conditioned room surrounded by walls of written wonder.

Why wait for her English teacher to assign the books? Anne got a head start with *The Catcher in the Rye*, *Fahrenheit 451*, *To Kill a Mockingbird*, and *Lord of the Flies*.

A month into the semester, by the time she finished the last page of that stack, she'd lost much of her faith in humanity.

She perused the shelves to find one of her old favorites: *The Lion, the Witch and the Wardrobe*. When her fingers brushed against the familiar binding, she pulled out the book and with her head down, rounded the stack of shelves, bumping into someone in the aisle.

"Steve?" She hadn't seen him in the library, ever.

"Sorry," he said. "I didn't see you."

"I didn't know you liked to read." She gave him a sideways glance.

He shrugged sheepishly. "Read more than I watch TV."

She understood and did the same. "I never run into you here though."

"Wasn't trying to run into anyone."

She raised an eyebrow, said nothing, and took her book to the table.

He followed and sat across from her. "Why do you hang out in here?" he asked.

"Same as you it sounds like. I don't want to be seen." She leaned closer and lowered her voice to a soft whisper. "The girls here are mean."

He frowned and nodded. "Yep. Guys, too."

"You're a senior. You shouldn't have to worry about anything. Besides, where's your girlfriend? I thought you were going steady with someone."

He slouched into his seat.

Heat rose to her cheeks. "I'm sorry. Did I say something wrong?"

"She broke up with me for some jock."

"That's her loss then."

Steve gave her half a smile. "Thanks. Nice to hear someone has that opinion. In case you hadn't noticed, we stick out around here."

"We?" Anne glanced around. "What do you mean?"

"Don't tell me you haven't noticed."

"Noticed what? Oh, right." She pictured Linda and her clique. "I don't dress as nice as the other girls."

"It's not that," he said. "Although I think you dress very nicely. We're a bit too country for these folks."

"Country? What are you talking about?" She held her head high. She'd been a typical Beverly Hills princess when she grew up. These girls had no idea.

"Ever watched the new show on TV?" he asked. "*The Beverly Hillbillies?*"

Aghast, she opened her mouth in silence at a loss for words.

"Exactly," he said. "That's how they view us."

"That's not fair," she said. "I've got way more class than that. I'm *from* Beverly Hills for God's sake."

"Shh." He leaned forward and held his finger to his mouth. "I know that, Ms. High and Mighty... I'm joking."

"Well, it's not funny."

"I am serious about the difference between us and them though. They don't wake at the crack of dawn to feed chickens and goats. Most of them have never ridden a horse. They get their eggs from a market. We're not the same as them."

A dread came over her. "I want to go home. I wish we didn't have to go to school here."

"Stop it," he said. "You're not here for them. You're here for you. Someone as smart as you should go to college and have a career. You don't need to work on the ranch all your life."

"Of course not. Why would I?" Even as she spoke the words, guilt gnawed at her for even thinking them. She'd be ashamed if her grandpa heard her.

"It's okay to dream about leaving the AV and still appreciate things here at the same time." He shrugged. "As for me, I'm not as smart as you. I'll probably end up working for your grandpa forever."

If she were any closer, she would've slugged him in the shoulder. "No, you won't. One day you'll own your own ranch. If that's what you want to do."

He motioned around him. "Don't know what I want but I don't fit in around town."

This saddened her. Steve was stronger, sweeter, and handier than any of the guys on campus. Definitely more handsome.

She blushed and bowed her head to hide behind her hair.

"Guess I'll leave you alone," he said. "That's a good book."

She glanced up and her eyes met his. "You're welcome to stop by and visit anytime, Stevie."

He narrowed his eyes and pretended to scowl. "Watch it, Ms. Anne D."

They laughed. A woman at the end of the aisle shushed them. They peered at each other and suppressed their giggles.

Maybe life in AV wasn't so bad after all.

8

Outlaws

THE REST OF ANNE'S FRESHMAN YEAR went by in a blur. She focused on her studies, which kept her distracted from her self-enforced separation from other students. After he graduated at eighteen, Steve began working for her grandpa full-time. One night in August, over dinner, her grandpa eyed her with suspicion and a mischievous smirk.

"What?" Anne asked. "Why are you looking at me like that?"

He finished chewing his burger and wiped his mouth. "Did Steve ask you yet?"

"Ask me what?" She tried to act annoyed but awaited the answer with eager anticipation.

Her grandpa sipped his water and gave a dramatic pause before continuing. "On August 23, they're having a grand opening for the first part of the 14 Freeway. 'Course it's not open for a few more months and even then, it won't make its way out to the AV for a couple more years."

She leaned forward on her elbows. "What does this have to do with Steve?"

"He asked me if you could join him in attending the ceremony."

She glanced down to mask her excitement and tempered her voice. "That would be nice."

"Hmm…" Her grandpa stared at her for a moment before getting up to clear his plate.

Steve borrowed his dad's truck and picked Anne up early that Friday. She put on her best dress—a plaid fit and flare dress belted around the waist—and her dressy flats. The sun beat down in the few minutes it took for her to cross the gravel driveway. Steve opened the passenger door for her. Was he being polite or more than that? She climbed up.

As they headed west into town, then south through the mountain pass, Steve acted as her informal tour guide.

He pointed off to the side of the road. "The San Andreas Fault runs right through here."

Bemused, she nodded. "Mmhmm. That's neat."

"Most of the time, major fault lines aren't visible; they're not painted on the dirt like the stripes on a road," he said. "But you can spot places where the earth is layered. See there?"

Since when did he become so academic? She smiled. Was this his nerves talking? She hadn't known Steve to be anything but confident.

They rode in silence until he spoke again. "Up over there is the town of Agua Dulce, sweet water as it was named by Spanish missionaries."

How did he learn all of this? Was he making it up as he went?

He continued, "It's up near Vasquez Rocks where the notorious Californio bandit Tiburcio Vasquez hid out." He gave a dramatic pause. "Until he was hung in 1875."

She rolled her eyes. "That sounds pleasant. Can we go there next?"

"Sure," he said, "we can stop by after the ceremony."

She faced forward. Obviously, her sarcasm was lost on him.

When they arrived, they found the highway overpass lined with over two thousand people. A helicopter hovered overhead. This was a bigger deal than Anne had realized.

Beauty queens, including Miss Antelope Valley, posed for pictures with men in suits.

Anne glanced at Steve. To his credit, he was not staring at them.

The highlight of the day's festivities was the dramatic moment when beauty queens held the ends of a ribbon strung across the width of the freeway. An official sliced it in half while a helicopter flew low and hovered overhead.

Anne squeezed her eyes shut, afraid of the helicopter crashing.

The sun scorched her skin and sweat glistened on her arms.

Steve escorted her back to the truck.

"Wasn't that incredible?" He was excited as a kid in Charlie Brown's Market picking out fresh jerky and jawbreakers.

"It was, actually." She meant it.

When they drew near Vasquez Rocks, Anne peered out the window to discover a bizarre, angled outcropping of jagged sandstone. Collisions at the fault line, Steve explained, created these half mountains and shoved them up to the surface like a cluster of Titanic ships whose bows rise while their sterns sink. They had uplifted over twenty million years ago to point angry fingers at the sky.

"A lot of movies and shows are filmed out here," he said as he helped her step down from the truck.

Her shoes were covered in dirt as were her legs. She tread carefully along the rocky ground to prevent twisting her ankle. A dress and her dressy flats were clearly not the appropriate attire for exploring mounds of boulders.

"Guess you can't get very far in those shoes." He pointed at them. "I can carry you on my back."

"Is that the best idea while I'm in a dress?"

He laughed. "I suppose not." He reached for her hand and guided her to a shaded area where they could sit. "Hold on a moment." He jogged back to the car and reappeared with a jean jacket. He laid it out on a flat rock and invited her to sit.

"That was a very gentlemanly thing to do." She curtsied. "I'm much obliged."

"Anything for the lady." He gave her space and sat a few feet away.

"Why are you acting so strange?" she asked.

He glanced down and shrugged. She observed his full lips and the stubble on his chin.

Heat rose to her cheeks. "I'm sorry. I didn't mean anything by that." She pointed at the distance. "These are different from the buttes back home. Rough surfaces but not as sharp."

With her praise, he perked up. "We can come back sometime if you'd like."

"Sure. When I'm wearing something more suitable, we can run and hide and pretend to be outlaws like Mr. Vasquez."

"Now that would be fun."

She fanned herself with her hand. "Sorry to be a bother, sir, but I do say it's terribly hot out and I'm flush with heat. The lady requests safe passage home."

He raised an eyebrow and held out his hand to help her to her feet. She gripped his arm to steady herself until they were safely back at the truck.

Not even a week later, Anne hid from the heat of the day in front of the television to view the March on Washington. A man named Martin Luther King Jr. delivered an awe-inspiring speech from the steps of the Lincoln Memorial.

She'd been to church before but never had a speech moved her to tears like his did. The Civil Rights movement was something talked about in history class and on TV. It was tragic what black Americans dealt with elsewhere in the country.

Thank goodness, the people in California didn't judge others based on race. For example, everyone on the ranch got along, regardless of race. When she told Steve that, he shook his head, called her naïve, and explained that not everyone was as accepting as she believed.

Without other friends to hang out with, she had nothing to compare the ranch to. The chickens and goats and horses treated people pretty equally. Whoever had the bigger carrot was the favorite, it didn't matter the skin color of the person holding it.

The preacher's voice and the lines in his "I Have a Dream" speech echoed in her head when she lay in bed at night.

It tore at her that people hated others for no good reason. Maybe if the people had a common thing to hate like the desert wind and the desert heat, they could rally around that and get over their differences. Her grandpa said she was oversimplifying things but didn't explain how. They left it at that.

Every person and every animal mattered to her, including those who couldn't stand up for themselves, especially Sage.

When she heard the news, Anne stomped into the barn and gave her grandpa puppy dog eyes. "You can't get rid of her," she said. "Sage stays."

"Are you paying to feed her?" Her grandpa latched the gate and turned to face her. "Duke, Piper, and Sienna are helpful. As for Gunner… he's strong." He pointed at Sage who had backed herself into the corner of her stall. "Her? How many horses do we need around here?"

Steve hoisted a bale of hay and carried it over to feed the animals.

"Let me at least try to train her," she said. "What do I do?"

Her grandpa shook his head. "Asking that question means you're not doing anything."

"I'll help saddle train her," Steve said. "Then, worst case, you'll get more money for a trained horse than a green one."

"Humph." Her grandpa shook his head. "The moment one of you gets hurt, she's gone. That's the only deal I'm making." He fanned himself with his hat and exited towards the orchard.

Anne stared down and dug the toe of her shoe into the dirt. "Thanks," she said.

Steve shrugged. "Your grandpa is right though. What are you going to do with another horse? How about another tractor? That would make his life easier."

"Why is everyone giving up on her?" she asked. "She's so sweet."

"Just because something is sweet doesn't mean it's needed. She may end up being a burden."

That stung. Her stomach cramped, and she blinked away her tears. She was a burden. That's how her other grandparents viewed her—as nothing more than a burden. Anne inhaled deeply, bowed her head, and hurried back to the house. Steve didn't stop her.

In the darkness of her room, lit only by the sunlight that streamed in through the edges of her closed curtains, Anne opened the dusty trunk at the foot of her bed. She lifted a blanket up and there, below that, she lifted out a photo album.

She settled into the corner of her bed and opened the cover. Mom and Dad—their wedding picture. Another page. Baby portraits of Anne. Her mom pushing her in a baby carriage in a park. Her toddling around their grassy backyard with the gazebo. She flipped the page. Her dad, hand-in-hand with her, strolled around a beautiful man-made lake built in the middle of a lush park surrounded by neighborhoods. Her dad holding her hands out, showing her how to feed the ducks at the lake— not Lovejoy Lake in the middle of the desert.

She flipped the pages. Her blowing out a candle on an elaborate princess birthday cake. Hugging the family cat. Snuggling alongside her mom, both nearly falling asleep on the couch. Anne ran her fingers along the bottom of the picture. Her mom's arms were wrapped tightly around her, and she nuzzled her head against her mom, a smile on both of their faces.

Anne closed her eyes. The scent of her mom's perfume, the warmth of her touch, the softness of her voice, her laughter. Goodnight hugs and kisses. Bedtime stories. Hot fudge sundaes at Wil Wright's corner ice cream shop. Her dad holding her hand in his and picking her up whenever her feet got tired.

She shut the photo album, shoved her face into her pillow and sobbed. She imagined herself like the outlaw Vasquez and imagined hiding out by herself in the remote hillsides made of boulders, never to burden anyone again.

9

Chasing Dreams

EVEN THOUGH ANNE DETECTED irritation under his efforts, Steve held to his word and trained Sage. The training meant Anne saw him around the ranch more, which made her happy, though she would never have admitted it.

Sophomore year in high school without Steve was painful. Anne determined it best to not get too close to anyone and kept potential friends at an emotional distance unless they lived out in Lovejoy or Wilsona, which eliminated all of her prospects.

She focused on her studies and read more books. A few guys wandered into the library during lunch and on occasion made flirty passes at her.

One day, a curly haired baseball player with freckles and a mischievous grin interrupted her silence. "You're keen on me, aren't you?" He smirked and glanced back over his shoulder.

Instead of feeling flattered, heat rose to Anne's cheeks and she fumed. Had other girls set him up to it?

"Not sure who told you that." Anne stared intently at the page in her book. The words blurred and she turned the page without reading it, hoping he'd go away.

"Is that a yes?" he persisted.

She sighed and glanced up at him. "I don't even know you."

"Sure you do. Name's Dave. I play varsity. And your name is?"

She raised an eyebrow, trying to judge his sincerity. "Anne. Thank you for stopping by, Dave, but I'm in the middle of something."

Instead of leaving, he turned a chair around across from her and straddled it.

"What are you reading?" he asked. "Where are you in it?"

She wasn't willing to be the punchline to someone's joke. On the other hand, she wasn't raised to be rude. Anne read the top of the page—she'd already forgotten the name of the book.

"*Where the Red Fern Grows*," she said.

Dave scrunched his eyebrows. "Haven't found any fern in the desert, much less red fern."

She closed the book and held the cover out to him.

"Oh." He laughed. "Is it any good?"

Better than this conversation.

She nodded.

"What's it about?" he asked.

"Are you honestly interested or just asking for the sake of asking?"

He laughed and nodded. "Yeah, I should let you get back to your book. Nice chatting with you, Anna. See you around sometime."

Anna? She sighed and opened her book. Even with Dave gone, she no longer could focus on reading. She peered inconspicuously through her hair as Dave exited the library. Sure enough, a couple of guys were out there laughing and giving him high fives.

On Friday, November 22, 1963, during Anne's English class, the world came to a halt. Her teacher ran out of the room next door in tears when word spread that President John F. Kennedy had been shot in Texas.

An announcement came over the intercom. The students and staff were sent home. Anne waited for the bus, surrounded by students sobbing. Their crying almost made her cry. Her chest and stomach tensed and she bit her lower lip. She never thought much of politics but the gravity of the situation was a weight that smashed everyone flat. She boarded the bus and paused in front of the driver. The older gentleman who greeted her every day with a kind smile avoided her gaze.

She slid into an open seat by herself. The boy across from her glanced at her with a tear-streaked face. This triggered something in her and she was overcome with a grief deeper than she thought herself capable. Her chest heaved and shoulders shook and she wept. Despair enveloped her as if she were eleven all over again. A cacophony of tears filled the bus until, overcome with exhaustion, silence overtook them for the rest of the ride home.

At her stop, she paused in front of the driver. He had bags under his eyes and the tracks of dried tears on his cheeks.

Without saying a word, she opened her arms and gave him a hug. When she pulled away, he gave her a sad smile and wiped tears from his eyes.

At the ranch, all work had ceased with the tragic news of the president's assassination. The TV news reported that Broadway had closed, and sports games had been cancelled. The scheduled programming was replaced with an endless news cycle. The young handsome face of the president smiling and waving before he was shot seared into Anne's memory.

JFK Jr., only three years old, stood beside the graceful first lady and saluted his dad at the national funeral. This beautiful image struck Anne. It was suffocating underneath the pain and unfairness of it all. How could a young child fully comprehend the death of his dad?

"Why would someone kill him?" Anne asked her grandpa as they sat glued to the television.

He shook his head, tears in his eyes. "Damn if I know. When something is ass-backward wrong in the world, it's fine for some narrow-minded folks so long as it's not wrong for them. And if good people try to make things right, folks destroy everything to keep what they got even if they got nothing."

Nothing else—not school, not the crops, not the bitter cold winds—mattered. Life was fragile and could be stripped away in a second. Her parents, like JFK, had lost their lives in a car. Were they also smiling like the president before it happened? Had it been quick like a shot to the head or did they suffer the last few moments? Did they look at each other in the final second?

Anne sighed. Filled with a comforting numbness, she had no more tears to cry. For days and weeks, the country was mourning. She felt as if her life were one big long extended funeral of mourning. Maybe her grandpa felt the same.

By the summer of 1964, Sage had mellowed. Anne's grandpa acknowledged as such and credited Steve with the progress despite Anne's frequent coaxing with treats and constant reassurances. She didn't care, relieved that Sage would be kept.

Thankful to be on break from school, she performed her errands with more cheer.

Early each evening, after she and Steve delivered the late afternoon feed to the animals, she retreated to the boulders beyond the barn to view the sun set and the stars rise.

"I'm heading out," Steve yelled out to her.

"Do you ever sit and stare at the stars?" she asked.

"Can't hear you." He approached. "What did you say?"

"The stars. Do you ever sit and watch them?"

"Who out here doesn't? They're hard to miss."

"Yes, they're beautiful. They're not this bright down below."

Steve shifted his weight. "You talk about down below all the time like you're just biding your time until you return."

"What do I have to return to? Nothing. What keeps me here? Nothing."

"What about your grandpa?" he asked.

"And when he's gone?" Almost immediately, she regretted saying this out loud.

Steve stared at her but didn't say a word.

"I'm sorry." She turned away. "I shouldn't have said that."

"Do you enjoy being miserable?" he asked. "Because you're really good at it."

"That's a mean thing to say. You try losing your parents and finding out that nobody else wants you. My other grandparents have a huge house with lots of money, and they refused to take care of me. They sent me away like I didn't matter."

"If that is what you dream about—money and a big house—you sure as heck ain't getting that out here." He sighed. "You can't live your whole life in the past. You need to think about your future. What do you want... *besides* not being stuck out here?"

She paused. "I haven't thought much about the future."

"Well, it's coming. You're going to be graduating in two years. What then? I can't picture you taking over the ranch."

"I suppose I'll go away to college. Then I'll do some type of miserable job in a beautiful town with trees and parks and streetlight-lined roads. Maybe I can get into the movie producing business like my dad and grandpa."

He chuckled. "I mean no harm in this, but you don't know the first thing about movies. And that sounds delightful—being miserable in a beautiful place."

"Better than being miserable in a wretched place." The sun lowered to a sliver on the horizon before disappearing. A trail of fiery oranges and reds spread across the sky, celebrating the end of another desert day.

"As if those are your only two choices." He shook his head and sighed. "I do hope one day you find what you're searching for—even if it's a miserable job in a town full of traffic, noise, and crowds. As for me, I choose this." He pointed to the sky. "Good night, to you, Anne."

Before she could say another word, he'd stepped away.

She stayed outside while the colors faded to pink then gray. The change in temperature was abrupt. Cool night air blended with the lingering heat of the day and blew across her skin.

A shooting star streaked across the sky. She tried to come up with a wish but Steve's words echoed in her mind. What were her dreams, besides longing for a life she no longer lived? Gazing up at the map of stars, Anne saw yet another place she couldn't navigate. And there went another shooting star. She took a deep breath, filling her lungs with the chilly desert air.

Peace. She wished for peace. Not world peace—highly unlikely—but inner peace, which was perhaps equally unlikely.

Could she find happiness and peace in a place where she never belonged?

In the autumn of her junior year of high school, Anne sat in class while a school counselor spoke to the students about their post-secondary options. Antelope Valley College, a local two-year community college in Lancaster, was an attractive option for those who hadn't decided on a career path or major or who didn't have the means to move away to pursue their dreams. At least that was Anne's interpretation of the lecture.

She left school that day more concerned than ever about what would happen to her after graduation. Grandpa Andy was sixty-one. Who would be taking care of whom soon enough?

Far more questions than answers swirled. She wasn't prepared for the future and was acutely aware of that fact. Nagging guilt and fear overtook her when she settled into bed at night. A clock constantly ticked and the ticking was speeding up.

After Christmas, with its usual tinsel-covered tree, Anne sat and stared at the string of colored lights before bed. Her grandpa had already retreated to his room.

Something was missing but she couldn't name what it was.

She brushed her hair and snuggled underneath the heavy quilts, which helped protect her against the icy chill that radiated through the wall and window.

Then it hit her. Nana and Grandpa Dougherty—her dad's parents, the grandparents who sent her away, hadn't sent a card with money. Maybe the mail was especially slow this holiday.

No. Come to think of it, they didn't send her a birthday card last year, either.

An uneasiness crawled through her body.

10

Premonition

HESITANT TO WORRY HER GRANDPA, Anne chose not to verbalize her concerns. As her seventeenth birthday approached in the spring, she checked the mail daily.

Chuck's wife, as she'd done annually since Anne's arrival, came over with Chuck and Steve and a freshly baked German chocolate cake.

A new sweater and book bag from her grandpa. No card from her dad's parents.

She searched in the trunk at the end of her bed for the card they'd sent her the prior Christmas. The writing was jagged, the signature like scribbles. In haste to cash the check, she hadn't paid attention to the degradation in writing quality.

She pulled out the leather address book which had belonged to her mother. She held the binding up to her nose, hoping to detect the scent of her mom's perfume. All that remained was dust.

She made the long-distance call to her grandparents, which she hadn't done before. A machine clicked on with an unusual chime and a message: "We're sorry. You have reached a number that has been disconnected or is no longer in service." Her heart dropped. Another link to her past disconnected.

She relayed the situation to her grandpa over dinner.

Her grandpa sighed. "Not surprised, Anne. If I remember correctly, they were born back in the early 1880s. Your dad was quite a bit older than your mom."

Anne flashed back to her parents' funeral. The church. The caskets. The tears. The prayers. Everyone dressed in black.

"Who arranged all of that for them if they died?" she asked.

"Funerals are for the living, not the dead." He buried his head into his hands. "God knows I've held too many of them."

While collecting eggs the next morning, she told Steve while he fed the horses.

Steve wiped his face with a neckerchief. "How do you feel about that, if they are gone?"

"How should I feel?"

"There's no should or shouldn't. The feeling just is or isn't. Not sure how much of that you can control."

She lifted the basket of eggs. "I've got no one left except my grandpa."

"Were you close to them?"

"No." Then again, was she close to anyone? Had she ever been?

"I think it's time you check out the lake," he said.

"That's an odd thing to say." She stared at him, wondering if he was just trying to change the subject. "Why would I go to the lake?"

He shrugged. "Why not?"

Her usual excuse, that it would remind her of her mom, felt as stale as last week's bread. "Fine," she said. "Let's go."

Rather than take the horses or the truck, Steve suggested they walk to take advantage of the pleasant spring weather that was neither scorching hot nor blistering cold. She packed some pears and sandwiches while Steve filled their canteens and told her grandpa that he'd have her back before dark.

When they rounded the outer edges of Lovejoy Buttes, clusters of cottonwood trees appeared. They were the same trees that lined the wash which wound down from the San Gabriel mountains through the desert, the natural path of the occasional flash flood.

The bright blue sky framed the orangish-brown rocky buttes. Green canopies of trees encircled the dark blue water of Lovejoy Lake.

"It's beautiful." Anne gasped in wonder as they approached it. "All these years… it makes me sad."

Steve billowed a blanket and set it down under the shade of a tree. "Because of your mom?"

"No, because it doesn't remind me of her at all."

He sat down on the blanket and took a swig of water. "Please explain. You said she brought you here to fish when you were little."

Anne stood, her eyes transfixed on the placid water. "She did." She returned to sit beside Steve. "I wish I could have a house right here, underneath these trees next to the lake. It's gorgeous. And to think all this time grandpa owned this land and never built a house here."

"Three things." He handed her a sandwich. "First of all, he and another rancher split the land around the lake and the dam. Two, it's too marshy to build around here because the water levels have traditionally fluctuated along with the rainfall. Three, it's more like community property for people to enjoy. Like them." He pointed at a few boys at the other end fishing.

She took a bite of her bologna and cheese sandwich. "It's so lovely that I'm angry."

"Sad? Angry? You're making no sense." He leaned against the trunk of the tree and crossed his arms.

"It's like a delicious pie."

"That makes even less sense. Apple?"

"Peach," she said. "Warm delicious fresh out of the oven tasty treat of homemade peach pie. Everyone takes a slice, but I decline because I'm in a foul mood. Instead, I take a walk to be alone. When I finally return to the kitchen, the pie is gone. All that's left are brown sugar crumbs and a dried drizzle of peach glaze—enough to know how delicious it was and to regret missing out. Today is like that. It is clear to me that I've missed out on the joy of the lake for all these years because I was too stubborn."

Steve studied her and shook his head. "You're here now. The pie isn't gone."

They finished their lunch and took a stroll around the perimeter, careful not to step into the caked mud at the edges. Wind picked up and funneled dirt in the distance. She fastened her hair on top of her head and hurried to catch up with Steve.

"I've found arrowheads over here before," he said.

"Oh! Let's look for some." She scanned the area around her feet.

"It's not as if they're littered across the desert dirt for you to pick up. Native Americans used to live on these lands."

A crack in the distance made her jump. Overhead, the sky darkened.

"Surprise." He pointed in the distance. "A storm's moving in."

Another crack. The sky flashed with sheet lightning across dark gray clouds.

"Should we head back?" she asked.

Steve shrugged. "Probably get rained on either way."

Another crack and rumbling boom. More flashes of light.

She started toward the trees as if to seek shelter under them. He grabbed her arm.

"With lightning?" he said. With a dramatic cowboy drawl, he added, "Every now and then, Miss Anne, I'm reminded that you're not from around these here parts."

She rolled her eyes but said nothing.

"Who knows how much rain we'll get. Sometimes a lightning storm moves through with hardly any rain at all."

No sooner had he spoken than a deluge of fat rain drops showered down on them. The air was warm, the water the same. More booming thunder and bolts of thunder struck in the horizon. They hurried to gather up their things and walked back to the ranch while getting rained on.

By the time the barn came into view, the rain had ceased, and the clouds cleared. Blue skies resumed their rightful place, creating a protective dome over their heads.

She wiped her face with the blanket. "Well, sir, that was fun."

"Was it?" he asked. "Wasn't sure if the rain dampened things for you."

"Actually, it cleared things up nicely. I quite enjoyed it."

He looked at her closely, then smiled. She smiled back.

The present had finally become more interesting than the past. A welcome opening in her heart had presented itself. She wedged the day at the lake with Steve in the open slot.

There were not many comfortable days like that. In fact, by the time her junior year ended, Anne was already moping from the summer heat of '65. The reality of the desert resumed with the relentless sunshine and scorched dry air.

"Have you heard?" Steve whispered to Anne as they moseyed through the orchard to check on the pears.

"Heard what?" She glanced around. "Why are you whispering?"

"You mean your grandpa hasn't said anything? My dad won't shut up about it."

"About what?"

"The developers."

Overcome by the heat, she paused to take a breath. "Are we playing twenty questions?"

Steve raised an eyebrow. "I guess this shows how your grandpa feels about the whole thing."

She raised her voice. "What are we even talking about? What whole thing?"

"Shh." He did a 360-turn. "Strangers are coming around and talking about buying up the land for a housing development."

Anne burst out laughing. "In the desert? Who the hell wants to build houses out here? That's the most ridiculous thing I've ever heard."

"It's not funny," he said. "I'm dead serious. Some are talking about selling. My dad thinks if people are foolish enough to throw money at the farmers and ranchers for this land, that we should all take it and buy a place somewhere else with the cash."

"My grandpa would never sell."

"Not if my dad can convince him otherwise."

She narrowed her eyes at him. "Now you watch it. Nobody tells my grandpa what to do."

He held out his hands in defense. "Whoa. Calm down. I'm with you on this. I said my dad, not me."

"Well, I know nothing about it, so maybe it's not even happening."

"There's a community meeting Friday night at the elementary school. You should go."

She shrugged. "If Grandpa goes, I'll go."

"Oh, I'll bet anything that he'll be there. It's his land they want."

Anne said nothing to her grandpa about it, but over the next few days, heaviness bore down on the ranch; the atmosphere was filled with uncertainty.

11

Earth and Sky Alight

OVER DINNER ON THURSDAY NIGHT, Anne's grandpa cleared his throat to speak, something he never did when discussing how the day went or how she was doing in school.

Anne had her fork spun with spaghetti midair. She paused, trying not to miss his words on account of chewing.

The pitch of her grandpa's voice was noticeably higher. "There's a community meeting tomorrow night at the school. I'll be attending. We can have dinner earlier if—"

"Can I come?"

"To a boring meeting?"

"What's it about?" She set her fork down and leaned forward on her elbows.

"A lot of nonsense," he said. "The McGregory family is making a big deal out of nothing. Well, them and some others."

"McGregory? He abandoned his wife and kids a few years back. What do they have to do with anything?"

"I wouldn't say he abandoned his kids. He did them a favor by gifting them with his absence. Now the three boys are old enough to have families of their own and they don't want to stay out in Wilsona. They want out and they're willing to destroy Lovejoy to do it."

The more he spoke, the more confused Anne became. Wilsona and Lovejoy were two neighboring communities. How could one destroy the other? She raised an eyebrow.

Her grandpa sighed. "If you ask me, they're the ones who started the whole shenanigans. They got the Haltons on board and that's where we got a problem."

"The Haltons?" They owned the land adjacent to her grandpa's. They dry farmed—not too successfully as her grandpa would argue—and kept to themselves.

He continued, "Who knew having Halton Ranch next to Hoffman Ranch would confuse the hell out of some two-bit swindlers. Sure beats me."

"Grandpa, is someone trying to buy your land?"

"Over my dead body."

"The Haltons or McGregorys?"

"Who said either of them wants this pile of dust?"

"Then who?" she asked.

Rather than answer, her grandpa stood up and carried his dish, still half full, to the sink.

"You didn't finish eating," she said. "Aren't you hungry?"

"Eating food is a waste of time. The more time you waste eating, the more time you waste in the bathroom."

Her eyes widened. She didn't press further.

On Friday night, she made sandwiches for dinner. Even though her grandpa repeated that he wasn't hungry, she made sure he ate. Clearly, something else was eating at him.

As soon as the two of them headed from the truck across the parking lot toward the meeting, they could hear shouting. The crowd was cantankerous. Anne couldn't make out what was being said with multiple words being yelled at the same time.

Her grandpa held his head high and led her into the building. The moment he stepped through the door, the room came to a hush. All heads turned toward him. Rather than take a seat, he leaned against the back wall and folded his arms.

"Go on and take a seat," he whispered. "No sense in both of us standing."

What was the point in either of them standing? There were open seats.

Steve waved at her from the back row and Anne settled into the chair next to him. His dad, Chuck, was in a crowd of other men, including the Haltons, up near the front. Across from them were another group that included the McGregorys.

Her grandpa kept watch from the back like a hawk scoping out its prey.

"Well, look who the cat dragged in," the eldest McGregory boy chided. A man in his mid-twenties, he wore an ancient pair of jeans pulled taut by a large belt buckle that on him appeared small. He rubbed his forehead as if he'd had a headache all day.

"Now, there's no need for any of that," said Mr. Halton, a lanky man whose gray hair was tied back in a long ponytail. "We're all friends here."

Snickers and jeers rolled through the room.

"I've known Andy Hoffman since we were boys," Mr. Halton continued, "and I think we should listen to what he has to say about the whole thing. Andy?"

"G'evening to you, Halton." Her grandpa tipped his invisible hat. "Nice turnout I see."

"Stop being coy," the McGregory boy said. "You know damn—"

"We got ladies in the house," Halton said. "It wouldn't kill you to be cordial. Andy, I ain't going to apologize for him. That's his mom's business—"

Laughter rippled through the room. McGregory's face turned red. He narrowed his eyes, chewing with his mouth shut as if he were rolling marbles in his mouth.

"What's all this about?" Anne whispered to Steve.

He turned and whispered back, his breath warm against her ear and neck. "A couple of suits were here last time and made a presentation about creating some lake community with housing tracts. McGregory and Halton and some others, my dad included, want to sell before the developers change their minds. Others want to hold out for a higher price. While another group, your grandpa included, don't trust the buyers and aren't interested in selling."

People shouted back and forth.

Anne leaned close to Steve, her lips almost touching his skin. "So why don't the ones who want to sell now go ahead and sell and leave the ones alone who don't want to?"

"It's all or nothing with the developers. They're planning a lake community. Your grandpa holds the other half of the land around the lake. A bunch of the guys here don't own land around Lovejoy Lake, so they'd only benefit from the offer if your grandpa sold."

"Where would the people go if they sold?"

"That's just it. Some of these people pushing for a sale have only an imaginary plan of what they'd do and where they'd go."

She settled back into her seat and crossed her arms.

"Andy's family is one of the original ones out here," Halton said. "His opinion matters."

"Well?" McGregory shouted at the back of the room. "What you got to say, Andy?"

The room silenced. Every head turned to face her grandpa.

Still leaning against the wall with arms crossed, he shook his head. "It's a fool's errand. We don't know these outsiders and I don't trust them. You all believe they'll preserve the lake as is. How is it you missed their spiel about enlarging the lake, which for those of you who have been around a bit, you know that ain't going to work with the springs drying up... where's that water coming from? Then installing a fancy restaurant at the end of the dock, which none of us will be able to afford, and adding jet skis and boats."

He pointed at a couple of teens towards the back. "There goes your fishing." He pointed at a couple of women in the middle. "There goes your quiet way of life. Add in some streetlights, cut through the desert with a bunch of roads, and what do you got?"

He motioned at the ranchers and farmers towards the front. "For those of you who plan to stay, what makes you believe you're going to share those water rights? You get cars and people in here and we turn into a city, a city far from a highway. They're almost done with the 14 freeway. People want to live near that, not out here in the middle-of-nowhere. Then what? A bunch of vacant properties. The living out here is tough—the winds, the heat and cold. Not exactly the oasis for the city folk that the developers are selling it as."

He pursed his lips and sighed. Then he added, "For all of these reasons, I'm not selling."

A firestorm of criticism, grumbles, and arguments broke out. Anne's grandpa pointed at her and gestured that they were going to leave. She whispered goodbye to Steve and hurried to the back. Her grandpa sauntered out in no hurry, ignoring the taunting and jeers.

After he turned on the ignition and headed back onto the road, he spoke to her. His voice was calm and tinged with sadness. "They're willing to trade seventy acres of working land for one acre, their parents' houses for a shoddy one identical to their neighbors,' all thrown together in identical rows without anything except a rectangular plot of dirt between them."

"When you put it like that," she said, "what's in it for the others?"

"They assume they're going to get rich." He exhaled. "They don't know the first thing about money if they think pennies on the dollar will amount to much of anything."

She stared through the windshield at the dark bumpy dirt road as they turned off the street. "Maybe they're tired of living out here."

"What would their parents say?" he asked.

Anne eyed him with curiosity. "Why would that matter?"

"We don't make it where we are, good or bad, without help from them." He drove under the gateway, pulled up around the back, and parked. The headlights shone on the dust cloud as it slowly settled back down to earth. "It's something to consider, the sacrifices others made on our behalf. Staying put is a way to honor that and to honor them."

She kept quiet. She wasn't beholden to anyone.

Anne slept fitfully. In the middle of the night, a commotion broke out, dogs howling and barking, neighing horses, bleating goats and wild sounds of chickens. Initially, she thought she was dreaming until her grandpa threw open her bedroom door.

"Get up and get dressed!" He screamed, already turning to go.

In a blur, she threw on jeans, a jacket and sneakers and ran outside. In the dark of the night red flames licked the sky. Contrary to her instincts, she ran towards it, following her grandpa.

That's when realization hit her. Their barn was ablaze.

12

Inferno

"GOD DAMN IT!" Anne's grandpa screamed. "I'll get the animals out. Call for help!"

The roof of the barn crackled. Fire twirled in circles. Black smoke billowed up into the sky, blocking out the stars. Her grandpa disappeared around the back of the barn. Panic gripped Anne. Her heart pounded. She sprinted at full speed through the moonlight, lunging over rocks and weeds, to the front of the barn. The doors were already wide open. She inhaled smoke and coughed spasmodically, her face warm from the heat.

The dogs ran in circles and barked at the fire and at the goats who stupidly stood there until they were chased away. Chickens were everywhere.

Sage. Sienna. Where were the horses? Anne stood there stunned.

A large piece of timber cracked and fell in front of her. She jumped back. Where were the firefighters? Shit. She was supposed to be calling for help.

Blinded by the fire, she raced back to the house in darkness, sobbing with worry for her grandpa and the animals.

With shaky hands, she dialed zero for the operator and was connected to the fire station. They assured her that they'd be there as soon as they could. Did they need an ambulance?

"No," Anne said. "At least I hope not."

She dialed Chuck's number and Steve answered half asleep. When she breathlessly relayed the situation, he said to stay put. They'd be there in minutes.

She had no one else to call. More than ever, she longed for her mom and dad.

Her grandpa. Where was he?

When she stepped outside, the view took her breath away. What had started as a fire was now an inferno. Pushed back by the heat, she couldn't get close.

"Grandpa!" she screamed. What if he were trapped inside? "Grandpa!" she yelled repeatedly as she circled the barn. The cracking and snapping of the burning wood engulfed by the roaring fire was deafening.

For a long moment, the world beyond disappeared. Her eyes were transfixed on the blaze. She was alone in the no longer silent desert, her and the burning barn.

Part of the roof collapsed, shooting sparks toward her. She jumped back. An ember landed on a dry weed. She jumped on top of it, twisting her foot back and forth to snuff it out before it took life. Another ember alighted a twig of dry brush.

She kicked dirt at it, got closer, and shoved more dirt.

Another weed caught fire. She stood paralyzed in place. A breeze blew and lifted embers up and littered them across a creosote bush.

No. Not the wind.

She jumped back, disoriented by the heat and smoke and burning chaos.

"Grandpa!" she screamed again into the dark void. Her eyeballs felt scorched from the heat. Shouting from far away grew closer.

Two hands grabbed her by the arms and pulled her back. She swung around, face-to-face with Steve. The fire reflected in his eyes.

"Where's Andy? Where's your grandpa?" he yelled.

"I don't know," she said. "Help me find him." She grabbed Steve's hand to pull him towards the barn.

"No." He yanked her away. "Get back. The firetruck is here. Let's get out of their way, so they can save the house."

The house. Her photo albums and whatever mementos she had left from her parents.

"Come with me," she said. "Help me save our stuff."

Steve nodded and led her through the darkness. A crowd of neighbors had gathered round. Word had spread almost as fast as the flames.

Firefighters drove a couple of engines up and doused the barn and the desert around it.

She paused and coughed, gasping for air, unaware she had inhaled so much smoke. What happened to the animals? Where was her grandpa?

Her heart sank.

13

Broken

THE WORLD WAS CHAOS. Anne froze in place, her face turned toward the flames, far enough away to no longer be hit by the heat. Instead, the cold desert air stuck to her clammy skin. People around her shouted and pointed at the remains of the barn.

She was invisible to the world.

"Anne?" Steve nudged her. "Anne, are you okay?"

She blinked. His voice was far away as if she were sinking underwater.

The desert before her disappeared. She was back in her old house in her lush backyard, hiding in the gazebo. Ivy had grown up around all the posts. Blooming star jasmine. That was the scent emanating from the delicate white flowers hanging around her head. The stone bench was cold. She didn't care. The babysitter, a college girl from her neighborhood, had been shaking her.

Police had shown up when her parents didn't arrive home at the time they'd promised. They always came home when they promised, until the night when they didn't. They departed the restaurant. The *idiot* ran a red light. Turned out the *idiot* had his own problems—alcohol being one of many, such as caring for a wife with cancer.

The sitter shook Anne again and kept yelling her name, alternating between begging, syrupy sweet with kindness, and frustration. The sitter and the officers used words like *catatonic* and *she's in shock* and *are you sure there isn't anyone else for us to call?*

She does have grandparents.

"Anne?" More shouting. Hands gripped her arms and shook harder. "Anne? Can you hear me? Do you know where you are?"

She blinked. She was back in the desert with her grandpa's barn burning in the distance.

It wasn't the babysitter. It was Steve.

She nodded, unable to speak.

"Come with me," he said. "Your grandpa's waiting for you. They're trying to convince him to take a ride in the ambulance to get checked for smoke inhalation, but he's refusing. He wants to speak with you."

She was floating. Steve, with an arm around her shoulders, guided her back to the house.

Paramedics were in the living room administering oxygen to her grandpa, who leaned back in his recliner. When he spotted Anne, he tore off the mask and coughed.

"Where...have you... been?" He coughed some more. "Worried..." He wheezed and coughed and shook his head. He allowed the paramedic to replace the mask.

"I'm so sorry." Anne kneeled beside him and held his hand. "I thought you were stuck in the burning barn."

Her grandpa shook his head again. He squeezed her hand tightly twice then didn't let go.

By morning, the ashes had settled and hot spots were extinguished.

Nobody had to wait for a grand investigation. It was arson. They all knew it. No one 'fessed up to having any evidence about *who could've done such a thing*.

Accusations were thrown around like rocks with most of them landing at the feet of the McGregory boys. They adamantly denied it. Ma McGregory was furious that anyone would dare to make any accusations about any of *her* boys. What with her lousy husband's history, no one had the heart to push her about her obliviousness.

The Haltons and other families, including Chuck and Steve, helped round up the horses, sheep, and goats—all of whom had survived—and offered to house them temporarily. They separated the animals between three ranches because no one had enough stalls available for all five horses—Gunner was enough trouble on his own to merit him being the only charity case one family could handle.

Not all the chickens made it, but that didn't matter as much to her grandpa as his independence, which had been burned to the ground.

Mr. Halton pulled Anne aside. "You keep an eye on your grandpa for me. I've never seen him like this. 'Course it's understandable." He paused and took a slow, deep inhale. "Andy and I go way back, back before he lost the babies, and his wife, and then your mom. This, though, I think this could break him." Halton had not said this much to Anne in the five and a half years since she'd lived there.

"I will," she said. "I don't know what we're going to do though without the barn."

"To be honest, he's got more coming from the crops and the orchard than he makes with all those mouths he's been feeding. And the land is worth more—"

She widened her eyes and stepped back.

Halton took his hat off. "I didn't mean it like that. Those animals are his family, too. All I'm saying is that financially, he could still be all right. I didn't want you to get worried about that part of things."

"My grandpa doesn't have a mean bone in his body," she said. Her body tensed up and she balled her fists. "Someone did this to him. They need to pay for this."

Halton opened his mouth. Before he could speak, Steve showed up.

"Hey, Mr. Halton, need help with something?" Steve brushed the dirt from his hands.

Halton returned his hat to his head. "Nope, that should be it for today. We'll have to talk soon, to make arrangements." He stared over Anne's head at Steve. "Folks don't have a ton of extra money lying around for feed. We'll all do what we can, though. That's what the community is for. We help each other out." He tipped his hat at Anne and departed.

"What was that about?" Steve asked.

She sighed. "No one really cares, do they? They're all secretly glad it happened. It's all of their faults even if they didn't light the darn match."

Keeping her grandpa busy was the best course of action—Chuck and Steve agreed as did the other ranch hands who showed up to help clean the debris. It was slow work. The men kept pushing her grandpa to go tend to the crops or the orchard, rather than stay there to witness the removal of every horseshoe and rail post—each item older than Anne.

Her academics suffered. Thankfully she passed her finals which kept her grades afloat and kept her busy until summer.

Her grandpa hadn't been the same since the barn burned. Anne cheered him like a toddler encouraging him to watch TV in the evenings. Truth was neither of them cared about cooking or meals. Dinner became yet another chore.

Chuck's wife would send over food at least once a week, stew or pasta or pot roast. At the rate Anne and her grandpa ate, the leftovers carried them for several days.

A few other neighbors occasionally dropped by a pie or a tray of beans and rice, sometimes tortillas and pork or chicken wrapped in foil. She and her grandpa thanked them.

Soon enough, neither of them spoke much beyond the bare minimum needed to get work done on the ranch and to pretend to care how everyone else's day was.

No one dared to ask them.

They didn't want to hear the truth because everyone already knew.

She and her grandpa were broken.

14

Like Magic

RINGLING BROS. AND BARNUM & BAILEY CIRCUS, a traveling three-ring circus, set up a Big Top in town. Elephants parading and ladies dancing on horses and amazing acrobats flying and tumbling and twisting through the air on giant trapezes—it's all anyone could talk about.

Even Anne and her grandpa perked up a little at the prospect of viewing something so far removed from their world.

Steve had gotten hold of a few tickets and insisted Anne and her grandpa go.

"Make a whole day of it," he said. "Get cotton candy, popcorn, the whole thing."

Anne cleared her throat. "That sounds expensive."

"How often does the circus come to town?" he asked. He whipped up their enthusiasm enough that, despite their misgivings, Anne and her grandpa cracked a smile and got to talking.

"It'll be a late night," Steve said. "My dad and Halton arranged for you both to stay the night up there with some friends. We all figured you both could use a break for a couple of days." Before they could protest, he continued, "Don't worry. Dad and I will check on the animals while you're gone. I'll feed the dogs. Go enjoy yourselves."

Although it felt a little like charity, Anne and her grandpa agreed they'd have a hard time arguing why people couldn't do something nice for them. It was their obligation to go.

They left early enough to get there with time to explore the carnival games and get suckered into viewing the three headed dragon, be enraptured by the magicians, jugglers defying death with flaming torches, and sword-swallowing freak shows.

Peanut shells littered the ground. They showed their tickets and ducked underneath the open tent flap into the dark interior of the Big Top. They found seats midway up in the packed stands. Her eyes adjusted to the dim lighting.

Her grandpa chuckled at the clowns who honked noses and horns and other antics, slipping and falling to the oohs, ahs, and laughter throughout the crowd.

The Ringmaster appeared in a spotlight in the center ring.

"Ladies and gentlemen and children of all ages," his voice bellowed through the loudspeakers.

The growling of the motorbikes circling around the inside of a locked cage, defying death with every rotation, the roar of the tigers who sat and moved on command, the crack of the whip as the horses pranced around the perimeter—Anne hardly knew she was holding her breath half the time until she gasped for air.

"Can you see that?" She pointed at the elephants on the far end.

"Not that old," her grandpa said, "still got good teeth, good eyes, and good sense."

Waves of disbelief spread throughout the crowd as one elephant after another stood on two legs, leaning the front two on the back of the one in front of it—a giant elephant row of dominoes.

In the shadows, lithe performers climbed rope ladders. After the animals left the tent, the lights focused on the trapeze artists and their gasp-provoking performances of midair summersaults and flips and grips and near misses. Her grandpa assured Anne the netting would catch them if they fell.

"They could still break their necks," she protested.

"Suppose it would be false advertising if it wasn't actually defying death, right?"

"Not funny." Yet, Anne was indeed smiling. By the end of the evening, her mouth hurt from smiling and laughing so much.

The next morning, they thanked their hosts—old friends of the community who had moved to town a generation ago—and prepared to head back to Lovejoy. Their hosts, an older couple who matched one another in height, stature, and temperament, insisted they stay for brunch and allow them to entertain them for the day.

Her grandpa nodded. "We appreciate it, but we've got to get back to attend to—"

"We won't hear any of your protesting, Andy," their host said. "Talked to Halton and all's well. We'll send you back well before dark."

After brunch, several rounds of horseshoes, another meal, and plenty of reminiscing about the old days, Anne and her grandpa were permitted to leave.

"Wasn't that something?" he said to her while their truck bumped along the rough two-lane road filled with cracks and potholes.

"Pretty incredible," she said. Wind blew through the open window and whipped her hair around. She had to yell to be heard. "Nice people."

"What did you think of the circus?" he asked.

The rest of the way back, they recounted the daring feats they'd witnessed, which became more death-defying and amazing with every retelling.

They passed Lovejoy Lake—no fence to indicate ownership, which she now knew was half her grandpa's. They pulled off the road, passed under the Hoffman Ranch gateway, and headed up the long gravel driveway that curved around the buttes. Before they reached the house, her grandpa brought the car to a sudden halt.

Up ahead, over a dozen cars and trucks that didn't belong there sat parked in the dirt clearing. Halton's faded red pickup truck led the pack, followed by cars belonging to most every family nearby in Lovejoy and Wilsona Gardens. Not a person in sight.

Her grandpa gripped the wheel. "What in God's name?"

"No one ever visits. Why are they here?"

"The mob has come for us. They couldn't get rid of me with the fire so they waited for us to leave to finish the job." He shook his head. "Maybe they think peer pressure will work, an intervention of sorts. Well, they thought wrong." He shifted into gear and crawled the truck forward. He parked beside the house and got out. His cattle dogs, Buck, Jesse, and Dusty gathered round, wagging their tails. "Didn't scare them off? What good are you?"

In response the dogs barked and ran circles.

Her grandpa put on his hat and marched forward, his boots kicking up dirt with every step. With hesitation, Anne followed closely behind, the dogs at their side.

They rounded the bend beyond the house and came to a halt. She nearly ran into him.

"It's not possible," he said. "I... I can't..." His voice choked up.

She came around his side. In the distance, on the footprint of soot where the former barn stood, was the skeleton of a pole barn. Over forty men and a few women labored in the hot sun. Beside them rested a tractor-mounted auger.

They had erected the framing, siding, and roof with trusses of weathered wood, planks, and sheets of metal, all supported by old telephone poles.

"God this must have cost a fortune." His voice quivered.

She took a trembling breath and wiped a tear. "They did this. They did this for you."

The dogs ran ahead in a flurry of barking. On cue, the work stopped, and every person turned in their direction. Steve jogged ahead to meet them halfway.

"Whose idea was this?" Her grandpa asked.

"This is incredible." Anne held her hand to her mouth. "How did you pull this off?"

Steve chuckled, took off his hat and wiped his brow. "Andy, you've been here for the community. It's about time the community was here for you."

For only the second time since she moved out there, she witnessed her grandpa sob. This time, his tears weren't rooted in grief.

"Looks like you can't sell now," Steve said. "Not with a new barn and all."

The crowd dropped their tools in place and gathered round.

"Nobody's got the money for this." Her grandpa wiped his eyes. "I can't repay you all."

"You already have," Halton said. "For every broken pipe and sputtering tractor and sick animal, you have given your time and energy for the rest of us."

Another man, Gordon from way down the road, stepped forward. "Advocating on our behalf with the county, helping me with my problems with property disputes, and with bookkeeping questions, it's me who should be thanking you."

Mom McGregory, an aged woman with weather-worn skin and dark under-eye circles, nodded. "When that no-good-husband of mine took off for good, you helped me and the boys trouble-shoot failed crops, gave me advice on wells and how to prune trees—you did what most people didn't." She eyed the people around her and settled her gaze back on him. "You saved our ranch. You saved me and my boys. And you never asked for a single cent."

"You've been racking up points people can't begin to repay." Halton sighed. "And the losses that you've suffered are more than most of us could bear to watch. This was too much. The fire… no one deserves to go out that way."

Neither Anne nor her grandpa could stop the tears. Their shoulders shook as Chuck's wife Marie came forward and embraced her grandpa. Steve did the same to Anne.

"Welcome home," Marie said. "Now before we get ahead of ourselves, let the men finish up the work while you two come in for a slice of fresh peach pie."

Steve gave Anne a final squeeze. He winked at her then returned with the others to the laborious task at hand.

Anne's grandpa wrapped an arm around her shoulder and guided her back to the house. "See? There is good in this world. Sometimes it takes tragedy to find it."

15

Secrecy

Anne's senior year in high school heightened her sense of uncertainty. On the one hand, life on Hoffman Ranch was back to normal, horses corralled, goats weeding to earn their keep, and missing chickens replaced. The alfalfa crops were healthy; the orchard produced the juiciest pears in several years. The community had backed away from cornering her grandpa with pressure to sell.

And yet, an underlying tension brewed beneath. Anne's future beyond high school was in limbo. Her grandpa had developed a slight limp from hip pain and Chuck dropped comments here and there indicating that land speculators and investors continued to tiptoe around the community without the advertised community town hall gatherings.

Whispers and side-eye glances behind her grandpa's back got Anne worried. Was the barn merely a distraction to placate her grandpa while gears of change churned behind their smiles and mundane greetings?

While picking pears with Steve in the fall, she probed him for answers. "Was building the barn a guilty act of goodwill?"

Steve wiped his forehead with a neckerchief, started to speak, hesitated, then shook his head. "Don't know."

She took a pear that had been pecked by birds and threw it off into the distance. "The hell you don't. Spill it."

He sighed. "I suspect, from what my dad mutters under his breath, that it was a way for neighbors to convince themselves that there's no harm in moving forward with the sale."

"The sale?"

"You haven't heard?"

She placed her hands on her hips. "When's the last time you've seen me communicate with anyone outside of the ranch?"

"People are selling." He glanced around in both directions and lowered his voice. "Why don't we take a hike up to the top of Lovejoy? It's a pleasant enough day."

"You mean the wind isn't hurricane level?"

After lunch the two of them walked the perimeter of her grandpa's property, staying close to the split-rail fence. Rather than ascend where they normally did, Steve led her further around to where the fence curved sharply and ended. Though it wasn't cold, he'd brought a light jacket.

Anne paused. "Why did we come this way? You've dragged me a quarter of a way around the buttes to make it harder on me?" She pointed to the edge of Lovejoy Lake in the distance and smirked. "Was this a ploy to get me back to the water? I didn't bring a swimsuit."

"No. I'm reminding you where your grandpa's fencing ends." He motioned at the butte. "Let's head up here."

The climb was steep along massive rough boulders. She watched her footing to avoid a twisted ankle.

"Love taking the harder way up," she said, huffing and puffing. "I mean why take a trail when mountain climbing is an option?"

Steve didn't respond. Instead, he led the way up. Every few steps, he turned and offered her a hand to help her navigate a large gap between boulders. Flowers sprouted between the cracks. Loose granules of granite made the surfaces slippery.

At last, they reached the top. Wind picked up and whistled around them. Her hair whipped in her face.

"Not a bad view, right?" he said.

She spun a three-sixty. Flat brown desert stretched in all directions, interrupted by the occasional butte that appeared more like a lump of rocks piled here and there. "A bunch of nothingness." Her eyes lingered on the violet-hued San Gabriel Mountains that stood proudly in the distance.

"Do you still wish you were on the other side of those?" he asked.

"Of course," she said. "Who doesn't?"

"Not everyone out here hates the desert." He took off his jacket and spread it out for her to take a seat.

"I don't hate it per se," she said. "Despise might be a better term." She raised an eyebrow and waited for his reaction.

"Despise," he repeated. "That's a harsh word."

"Why did you bring me up here?" She adjusted herself on the jacket and slid over to make room for him. "To tell me some secret that no one else can hear?" With a laugh she added, "You're in love with me. Is that what this is about?"

"I wish it were as pleasant a conversation as that. Besides, how could I love someone who despises the desert and everything—or everyone—in it?"

Her stomach tingled and she held her breath for a moment. "I don't despise everyone."

"I don't believe you."

"Take my grandpa, for example. I love him." She turned away. "You're not so bad either, I suppose."

"The princess approves." He laughed. "Why, I'm honored m'lady."

"Can someone who shovels horse shit be considered a lady?"

He nudged his shoulder against hers. "You do it in such a ladylike way."

She sighed. "What's going to happen to my grandpa and the ranch? I mean he's getting older. I can't take care of it by myself. It'd be nice if I had some help."

"What does help have to do with anything? Hired help can't remove misery."

A sudden gust plowed into them, making her sway with the wind. She leaned back on her arms to balance herself and squinted at the sunlight peeking through the clouds.

"What do you want?" he asked.

"The wind to stop. What do you want?"

He didn't respond.

She sighed and maintained her silence beside him.

"You know the developers are coming back around, right?" he said. "People are talking up some trickery."

"I figured as much, but what can they do if my grandpa won't sell? Maybe they can build their little development on Halton's side of the lake."

"How will they determine which side of the lake belongs to whom? Property lines aren't exactly marked with fencing."

She gasped. "They can't lie about that."

"Who can prove a lie if it's one word against many?"

She jumped to her feet and peered over the edge of the buttes in the direction of the clumps of cottonweeds and Desert Willows that surrounded the lake.

"They can't do that, can they?" She stared back at Steve.

"What do I know? I'm just the hired help."

"Knock off that stupid act. Be straight with me. How do you feel?"

"About the property problems or about you?"

She narrowed her eyes at him. "What's that supposed to mean?"

He strolled away from her and stood in silence gazing down at the lake.

Anne approached him. "Talk to me. Why does everyone always keep secrets from me?"

"What secret? I'm sure you already know."

"I'm done talking in riddles," she said. "I need you to be honest with me. Please."

He returned to his jacket and sat facing the mountains.

She settled back down beside him. "My grandpa's going to lose the ranch, isn't he?"

"I'll ask you again," he said. "What do you want?"

"For Sage and Sienna and Piper and Duke to be safe. Gunner can go to hell."

Steve chuckled. "Gunner is one stubborn stallion."

"And the dogs… Buck, Jesse, and Dusty need to feel useful. The goats keep them busy." She smiled. "And the chickens? Grandpa insists the hatching chickens go on display at the fair every year. As for the alfalfa… Me and the tractors never got along that well. I don't mind the pears though. The dirt? A minor complication."

He raised an eyebrow. "Minor?"

"And you? Well, you can be a real pain sometimes. But you can reach things that are too high up for me, so that's nice. I'd keep you around for that if nothing else."

He shook his head and laughed. "I've been reduced to a ladder."

She turned to him and smirked. His eyes delved into hers, only inches away. She breathed in a tiny gasp and studied his face.

He bent nearer and glanced at her lips. "May I?"

She nodded, shut her eyes, and raised her chin.

He wrapped his hands around her cheeks and pressed his lips against hers. The softness was warm and sweet as pie. She kissed him back. He pulled away.

"So now you stop?" she asked. "You asked me what I wanted. Stopping isn't it."

A warm grin spread across his face. He took her in his arms and kissed her again passionately. She put her arms around him, and they fell back onto the ground, her body on top of his. He brushed her hair out of her face and tucked a few loose strands behind her ears, brushing the back of his hands lightly across her cheek.

"Okay. This is absolutely what I want." She straddled him with a mischievous grin.

"Whoa." He sat up and carefully extricated himself. "Before all of that, I need to understand your intentions." He pointed to the mountains. "You're almost eighteen and ready to graduate. What then? Will you travel to a faraway place, and I'll never hear from you again?"

"There's nothing left over there for me." She regretted the words the moment she spoke them. She did want what was over there, but she didn't want to lose Steve. Her throat constricted. Steve had hope in his eyes, so she kept going. "I could be happy out here." She sat up and brushed her fingers alongside his bare arms and hands.

"With me?"

"Especially with you."

"What about the ranch though?" he asked.

She pointed in the distance. "What if we bought a place further out a bit, away from the disputed property, and we raised all the animals and cared for them together?"

"Are you proposing all of this as a 'we,' as in me and you?"

"I'm not proposing anything at all." She crossed her arms. "As far as I'm concerned, that's your job."

He beamed and leaned close for another kiss which she gladly gave. In the back of her mind, she wondered what it would take to convince Steve to leave the desert.

16

Proposals

IN THE EARLY SPRING OF 1966, the purr of a motor preceded the advance of a shiny blue Chevy Impala that kicked up dirt as it entered the ranch. Anne and her grandpa lingered on the porch as the car approached.

Anne glanced at her grandpa. "Who's that?"

"Someone who doesn't belong here." He crossed his arms and narrowed his eyes.

The car slowed to a crawl and parked in front. After the dust settled, two men stepped out dressed in belted slacks and unbuttoned polo shirts. With their slicked-back brown hair, tanned skin, and square jawlines, the only difference between them was the taller one had a scar that ran across his chin and a manila envelope in his hand.

They smiled pearly white smiles, too wide and too perfect.

"Mr. Hoffman?" The scarless one held his hand out to her. "I'm—"

"Trespassing," her grandpa interrupted. "Whatever you're selling, I'm not buying."

The men exchanged a glance.

The man with the scar stepped forward. He winked at Anne. "Not here to sell you anything, sir."

"Then what business you got here?"

"I've been given the liberty to make a very generous offer considering—"

"Offer?" Her grandpa snickered. "Get off my property."

"Andy, hear me out," the man without the scar approached with a disarming tone and a wide smile. "I'm not here to force you to do anything. Hoping we could sit down and you could at least entertain the proposal. If you don't like it, we'll leave."

"Who sent you here? Halton? Did he put you up to this?" When her grandpa's voice rose, the dogs appeared by his side and barked at the strangers.

The men took half a step back but maintained the grins plastered on their faces.

"Anne, is it?" The man with the scar motioned to her. "Can I give you something?"

"How do you know my name?" Anne said.

"Get the hell off my property unless you want to leave in pieces." Her grandpa pointed at the dogs. Detecting his mood, they barked louder and approached the strangers.

"Anne, catch," the man with the scar tossed the envelope at her.

Unprepared, she caught it.

The two men hurried to their car. The man with the scar motioned *call me* with his hand.

The dogs lunged on the car. The motor growled to life, the wheels spun in the gravel, and the car bumped down the dirt path and off the property.

Her grandpa chuckled as they drove off.

"What's so funny?" Anne asked, the envelope still in her hands.

"Boys like that won't appreciate the claw marks on their perfect paint." He whistled the dogs to follow him as he headed back to the barn. "They won't be back," he called out to Anne. "Toss that garbage."

She went inside the house. Her hand hovered over the kitchen trash. On second thought, she opened the envelope. A couple of business cards fluttered to the ground along with a note. A multitude of real estate forms were rubber-banded together, a transfer of deed, a typed offer for $10,000 in exchange for his seventy acres with land, water, and mineral rights. Ads in town advertised homes for $15,000. How could they offer her grandpa less than that?

She shoved the paperwork back in the envelope and dangled it over the trash. Before letting go, she slid a business card out and tucked it away in her pocket.

Anne settled beside Steve under a cottonwood tree at Lovejoy Lake. Wind whipped her hair around. She tied it back and unpacked sandwiches from her bag.

"You're eighteen on Friday," Steve said with a smile. "How does that feel?"

"It'll feel better in June after I graduate. School is exhausting." A sharp gust loosened her ponytail. She tied her hair back again, tighter. "I mean I'll enroll at AVC, but at least there I'll get to choose which classes to take."

"Glad you're sticking around," he said.

"To finish college." She quickly added, "With you here, where else would I go?"

"Hope that's not why you're with me... because there's no one else to date."

She blushed. "You know that's not true. I've decided you don't bug me as much as you used to."

"So, you're mildly tolerating me?" He laughed. "I guess I'll take that considering you used to throw pears at me and were only nice when you needed me to do your chores."

She shook her head and leaned against him.

"What do you think your grandpa will say about us?" he asked.

"He's always liked you."

"Maybe he already knows." Steve petted her hair and sighed. "Remember when we talked about working the ranch together with your grandpa? Is that still something you'd be happy doing... with me?"

She smiled at him. "Of course." She averted her gaze. Later on, Steve would understand if they had to move away, maybe for her career. At least she hoped that would be the case.

"He's not going to sell, is he? Everyone else is going to."

Her muscles tensed. "Not with the pennies they're offering him. Where would he go? And the animals? He's not going anywhere." She pointed to the trees around them, "He said they'd tear down all of this to make their big lake and houses. Then what?"

Steve brushed his fingers along her cheek and planted a kiss. "We won't let that happen." He cleared his throat and leaned back against the tree trunk.

"What's the matter?" she asked.

"Probably nothing."

"Probably?" She turned to face him. "What's on your mind?"

He sighed. "Water rights. What happens if Hoffman sells, the developers come in, and they siphon the shared water from your ranch? What then?"

She blinked in shock. Crops, orchards, animals, and people all depended on water. Without water, there couldn't be life.

Rather than worry her grandpa, Anne shoved these concerns to the back of her mind. She focused on finishing her classes. She'd deal with the rest later.

During a late afternoon in mid-June, while the heat of the day lingered, Steve pulled her grandpa aside for a private conversation. Anne eyed them with suspicion as she cleaned up the horse stalls. Her grandpa glanced back at her and nodded. He patted Steve on the back before they went their separate ways.

"What was that all about?" she asked when Steve returned to help her.

"Do you want to take a drive up to Wrightwood on Saturday?" he asked.

"For what? I have finals next week."

"I'll get you back early."

She put her hands on her hips. "What do we need to drive all the way up there for?"

"It's going to be miserably hot this weekend. It's not as hot up in the mountains."

"And that's worth wasting the gas?"

"It's not a waste if we have fun. We can take a hike under the pine trees."

She glanced around at the tumbleweeds blowing across the fields beyond the barn, the funnels of dust devils in the distance, and the blazing sun bearing down on the sparkling quartz in the buttes. She imagined the Joshua trees being replaced with tall pines and the dry, hot wind with a cooler breeze.

"All right," she said. "A break might be nice."

When Anne stepped out of the truck—Steve held her door open—she spun in circles in awe. The tops of the trees nearly blocked out the sky. She filled her lungs with the cool, clean air.

Steve held up a pinecone bigger than his hand. "Check this out."

Pinecones of various sizes littered the trail around her feet. She squatted down and admired the sharp prickles at the edges—not as sharp as Joshua tree thorns but still sharp enough to cut. A squirrel scurried up the trunk of the tree where another squirrel chased it further up.

Anne spun around and followed the path of a red-tailed hawk in the sky, which was far more graceful than the jets that zoomed overhead back home.

When the hawk disappeared beyond the tree line, she turned to find Steve kneeling down in front of her. Her stomach fluttered. He pulled a ring out of his pocket. She gasped.

"Anne," he said. "Would you marry me? I mean if you're willing to tolerate me long enough."

She stared at him and blinked. Her brain replayed his words until she could comprehend the question. Her heart raced and a grin spread across her face. She squealed. "Yes, Steve, yes."

He slipped the simple gold band around her finger, embraced her in a hug and lifted her in the air. "I promise, Anne, that I will always be kind."

The ring felt warm and comfortable, as if it was where it had always belonged. "Do I have to promise the same?" She laughed.

"Promise to be yourself. Which, honestly," he said, "is kinder than you'd like to admit."

Giddy during the drive back, they discussed possibilities for a summer or fall wedding.

"What about going back to Vasquez Rocks?" she suggested. "You liked it out there."

"Rather not start out where an outlaw lost. What about up in Wrightwood?"

"Maybe. Or even Lovejoy Buttes," she said. "Although it's hot and windy."

"Not a great way to start out a new life together," he said. "Getting blown off the buttes."

"But we'd be together." She smirked. "Wouldn't that be romantic?"

He shook his head. "Not quite how I'd define romantic. Then again, maybe I'm not reading the same books." He rolled down the window after they descended the mountain. The desert sun blazed hot on the glass. "There are plenty of options," he said, "and we have plenty of time."

Anne walked in her high school graduation ceremony. Afterward, she observed other girls run into the arms of their mom and dads. Flowers, cards, cheering. Hugs and kisses. She stared at one mom who embraced her daughter and posed while the dad took a picture. There were other graduates welcomed and congratulated by entire families of grandparents and aunts and uncles.

"Anne!" a voice shouted from the crowd. An arm waved.

There, as the people parted, stood her grandpa and Steve with a bouquet of flowers. She ran into her grandpa's arms and, despite trying her best not to, she cried into his shoulder. He wrapped his arms tightly around her.

"I'm so proud of you," he whispered. "I know your mom and dad are proud of you, too."

How was she supposed to feel? On the one hand, she was done. On the other hand, she'd been cheated out of the proud parent moment, the scene repeated all around her.

"I love you, my little Anne," he said. "I'm so glad I could be the one to share your joy with you here today. I'm the luckiest grandpa in the world."

A smile spread across her face. She closed her eyes and breathed in the scent of her grandpa's aftershave. "I love you, grandpa." In her mind, she added, please don't leave me anytime soon.

Steve was next with hugs and congratulations. He was her new beginning, the start of her new future. For the first time, she considered her current situation not only with sadness but also with hope.

The weekend after her high school graduation, while Steve and her grandpa worked the crops with Chuck and the other helpers, Anne washed up the dishes from lunch.

When she stepped outside, she scanned the horizon. A small cloud of dirt was headed in her direction.

She squinted into the distance. It was a car headed for the ranch. She glanced around. No one was left at the house except her.

A pale-yellow Cadillac drove up the gravel driveway and parked.

Not more of those good-for-nothing land developers. She crossed her arms.

A man in a suit stepped out—not one of the two polo shirts who appeared in an Impala several months back. This man was older and wore solemn wrinkles across his forehead and at the corners of his eyes.

Before he could speak, she shouted, "My grandpa isn't selling. You can take your offer, turn around, and leave."

The man didn't react. Instead, he opened his trunk and pulled out a briefcase.

"Morning, ma'am," he said. "With all due respect, I'm not looking for Anne's grandpa. I'm looking for Anne."

She froze. How was she involved in the whole mess?

"I won't entertain any offers or proposals from you," she said.

The man, unamused and unaffected, nodded. "Understood. I'm just doing my job, ma'am. I'm from a law firm. I have urgent matters to discuss. Can we go inside to speak?"

Anne scanned the area. No one else was there except her. She should get her grandpa.

As if detecting her hesitation, the man said, "I need to speak to you alone."

17

The Crux of It

ANNE SAT ACROSS from "just call me Ronnie" and listened to his spiel. The more he spoke, the less she heard. Her brain buzzed with nonsensical words like inheritance laws and estate plans and trust requirements.

Was this all a dream? Nothing he said could be real. She shook her head.

"Anne," Ronnie said. "Are you understanding the full implications of what I'm telling you? You haven't spoken a word."

She shrugged. "To be quite honest, I don't understand why you're here."

"Fair enough." Ronnie slid a stack of stapled papers across the table. "You are eighteen and have graduated high school, correct?" After she nodded, he continued, "This means you've fulfilled the requirements outlined in your parents' and your grandparents' trusts."

"What do these documents mean?"

"I am the attorney entrusted with executing their final wishes. Their estate is now yours. What you do with it is another matter entirely and one which you need to determine."

"So, this has nothing to do with you trying to buy my grandpa's ranch?"

"Now what ungodly reason would anyone have for buying a plot of desert dirt in the middle of nowhere? For God's sake, Anne, no."

She bristled. "This is my grandpa's ranch."

"Understood. And this," he said, pointing to the papers, "is your path back to civilization, back to Beverly Hills."

She gasped, realization setting in.

"That's right. You can leave this all behind." Ronnie smiled warmly. "You're inheriting a lot of money and a beautiful house. My firm can arrange for a car to pick up you and your things." He glanced around the room. "If there's anything you want to take with you for sentimental reasons."

"Why didn't anyone tell me about this? I didn't even know my grandparents died."

Ronnie widened his eyes and leaned back. "I sincerely apologize that you weren't notified of their passing." He cleared his throat. "As for the money, their wishes were for the matter to remain confidential and as such, you were not to be notified until after you satisfied the terms set forth in the documents."

Anne's mouth gaped open. Her throat constricted and tears welled at the corners of her eyes. A way out. A way back home. Home. The garden and gazebo. The grand staircase, her playroom with the giant dollhouse, the one with working lights and a doorbell thanks to her mom's handiwork. The living room with vaulted ceilings that let in the morning sun, skylights that held the last light of day where her cat napped on the floor. Her mother's fragrant rose bushes that lined the front path. The smoky barbecue in the backyard. She could go *home*.

She swallowed hard and found her voice. "My house? The one I grew up in?"

Ronnie flipped through the paperwork. "My understanding is that your former residence was sold seven years ago, shortly after your parents' passing. The money from the sale was set aside. Part went to charity. This is your grandparents' estate. Their house is yours."

Their house. The one with the cold marble staircase, the delicate tables that held delicate vases. *No running in the house.* The fireplace with the carved golden lions she was chided for touching. The yard where you had to stay on the stone path. *Don't run through the bushes. Stop tramping in the grass.* The family room with the cream-colored couches, the coffee table that always shined. *Watch your fingerprints.*

Oh. *That* house—the *no pets allowed* house. The one she hardly ever visited as a child. Her grandparents were happier trekking to her home where she couldn't break some priceless collectible. There was no warmth in the memory of their property.

"When would you like to take possession of the house?" Ronnie asked.

"What if I don't want it?" She leaned back in her chair. "I never much cared for their house or the things in it. I prefer the ranch." She was shocked at the words that had escaped her mouth, yet she didn't regret the sentiment. It felt true.

Ronnie's jaw dropped. "What on earth is worth staying out in this hellhole for?"

She glared at him.

He sighed and shook his head. "My apologies. I'm sure this has been overwhelming. Would it be best if we finalized things at my office next week?"

She could bring her grandpa and Steve to the house and make it a home.

"Can the horses come?" Her grandpa riding Duke, Steve riding Sienna, and her riding Sage—three horses tramping across the gardens. She giggled at the image.

Ronnie leaned his head into his hand and rubbed his temples. "Horses?"

"To the house."

"It's not zoned for horses. I suppose you could sell and purchase horse property, but I'd advise against it because of the negative tax implications."

"How much money is all of this?" she asked.

"Combined property and funds, your grandparents have it designed to keep you under the $60,000 estate tax exemption rate. The rest goes to charity."

Her eyes widened. "You're giving me $60,000?"

"Your parents left you some money as well. There have been a few lawsuits and claims from the production company your father ran. Everyone likes to dig their hands in the pot. We've done our best to defend against these claims. Can't say it turned out as well as I'd hoped."

"You brought the money with you?" Anne glanced at the briefcase.

"No." Ronnie sighed. "I most definitely wouldn't be handing you cash."

"But I still get all of the money?"

"After you sign the paperwork. Remember though that a large part of that value is in their property."

"Property?"

"Their house." Ronnie's face showed a strained patience wearing thin.

"I need to think about this. Can you leave the papers for me to read through and talk to my grandpa?"

"Very well." Ronnie stood. "Some advice for you, Miss Anne, if I may. It's best not to show your cards lest the vultures come calling."

She tilted her head. "What?"

"Maybe it's best you think it over on your own without broadcasting it to the world. Word spreads fast and you'll find you have more friends and cousins than you thought possible until the money runs dry." He rubber-banded the papers and handed them to her, snapped his briefcase shut, and stood to leave. "In simple terms, as your legal counsel in this manner, I'd strongly advise you not to discuss these matters with anyone other than me or a financial advisor."

"You don't know my grandpa—"

"I know human nature." He headed back to his car. Before getting in, he turned to her. "My business card is in the envelope. Call me when you've made a decision regarding the house or if you have any questions. If I don't hear back from you in a week, I'll contact you."

Anne stood on the porch while the yellow Cadillac returned its slow crawl back to the road, dust kicking up in its wake.

She hid the packet of papers in the chest at the end of her bed, on top of the business card from the land developers. Her mind floated above her head for the rest of the day. She kept tripping over her feet, unable to remain grounded in reality.

She brushed Sienna's mane and fed her a carrot. Sienna eyed her curiously as she mumbled to herself.

"What about you?" Anne asked. "Where would you and the other horses go if Steve and grandpa moved down below with me? It's a lovely place though, a huge house with a beautiful garden."

Tumbleweeds blew by in the fields beyond the barn, goaded on by the fierce winds.

"The weather is so much nicer down there." She wiped the sweat from the back of her neck. "I can't believe my good fortune. Steve and grandpa will be so excited. They won't have to work so hard ranching anymore."

Sienna whinnied. Anne blinked and realized she had stopped brushing her. She continued.

"What will grandpa do with his free time? Maybe he can birdwatch."

Turkey vultures circled the land beyond the buttes.

"Well, not *those* birds. I was thinking of hummingbirds and sparrows and whatever other kinds of birds there are. I suppose with his spare time he can learn about them all."

Sienna's ears pointed forward. She nudged Anne's face.

"Aww, sweetie. I don't know if you can come."

Sienna lowered her head and pressed into Anne's shoulder.

Over dinner, Anne twirled the spaghetti around her fork too many times.

"Not hungry?" her grandpa asked.

She snapped back to reality and glanced up. "Huh? Yes. I have a question."

"Shoot," he said.

"What would you do if you didn't have to ranch anymore?"

"I'll be dead six feet in the ground." He chuckled.

"That's not funny. I'm serious."

"So am I. I've never done anything but this. If I'm not doing this, then what use am I?"

"You're pretty important to me even if you weren't doing this," she said.

He sighed. "You hopping on the bandwagon of 'Let's convince Andy to sell?'"

"No, it's not that at all." She considered her wording before speaking again. "I mean what if me and Steve took care of the animals and you didn't have to work anymore. If you had all day to yourself, what would you love to do?"

He stared up into the distance and jawed his mouth a bit. "Figure I'd spend time fishing. Yep, just sitting on the bank of the lake fishing."

There wasn't a lake near her grandparents' old house. "What about a beautiful park or a garden? Would you enjoy sitting there?"

"Doing what?"

"Sitting. I don't know. Watching the birds. Relaxing."

"Fishing is relaxing. And I'd be doing something. I'd run myself up a wall if I had to sit there doing nothing."

Unless she set up a pond in the backyard, she couldn't figure out how he'd be able to fish in West LA.

"What about the ocean?" she asked. "Would you enjoy fishing at the end of a pier?"

Her grandpa laughed a hearty full-bellied laugh. "Trying to throw me overboard now, are you? No, I'll stay here where my feet are on the ground. The same ground where my parents lived and raised me."

"You wouldn't be happy anywhere else?"

"I have you and the animals and the land and the lake right here. That's all I need."

That night, Anne lay awake considering her options. What if she and Steve moved away? Her heart ripped at the thought of abandoning her grandpa here in Lovejoy. No, he needed her, like she needed him.

Maybe she and Steve could split time between down there and the ranch?

Back in high school, Steve remarked that the two of them were too country. The girls laughed at her. The athletes mocked her. Would Steve, with his cowboy hat and belt buckle and boots be out of place at her grandparents' estate? Could he be happy talking with the other parents about college plans for their children and hosting dinner parties like her parents used to?

A sliver of moonlight snuck in around her curtains and hit her in the face. She brushed aside the curtains. The night sky shone with stars against the darkness.

Down below, the stars were invisible.

She'd always dreamt of getting out of the desert. Here was her opportunity. Why did the thought of leaving hurt her heart?

She cursed the earth and sky and her parents for leaving her and her grandparents for ignoring her, and fate for forcing her out here. What should be a celebration of joy was a moment of impending doom. She had one week before Ronnie contacted her again.

What if Steve stayed and helped her grandpa and she got the hell out of there by herself? Would that be so selfish to do? She could build a new life for herself, get another cat, plant some rose bushes, add a gazebo to the backyard. That would be wonderful. Cool breezes, moderate weather, comfortable roads lined with streetlights.

If she took the money and the house, she'd have to leave behind both her grandpa and Steve. Her grandpa would be heartbroken to leave the animals and the ranch, so he'd stubbornly stay put. Steve promised to help him.

If Anne stayed out in this horrid desert with them—and she'd be out of her mind to consider such a preposterous choice—she'd give up her hopes and dreams of a happier existence and settle for mediocrity. This opportunity was everything she'd ever hoped for... the money, the house, the lovely neighborhood.

Is it what she really wanted? An easy life, or to love and be loved, to find peace.

The choices were incongruent. It wouldn't work perfectly either way.

18

Taking Flight

ANNE TWISTED A LOOSE THREAD on her jean shorts. She sat beside Steve in the shade alongside the barn to take a break from the morning heat.

"Something the matter?" he asked.

"Depends." Preparing to deny the truth, she paused. "If we could live anywhere, where would you choose to live?"

"Where we could afford to live." He shrugged. "Which I suppose means here."

"What if money wasn't a concern? Where do you dream of living?"

He folded his hands together and rested his chin. "I've seen pictures of ranches in Montana. Very green out there. They get rain and actual weather beyond wind."

"You'd still want to ranch, even if you didn't have to?"

"I love the animals and working the land, to bring life from dirt that feeds other life. It's an incredible thing when you consider it." He turned to face her. "Why do you ask?"

"Do you ever dream of not working so hard, of getting a nice house in a sensible neighborhood, a lovely place closer to the beach with better weather? No wind. Pretty parks and lots of trees. No snow. No day so hot it could fry an egg."

He laughed. "Sensible? What's a sensible neighborhood?"

"Paved roads for one thing. Sidewalks. Tree-lined streets. Maybe a hilltop view."

"That sounds anything but sensible. Would I have a Porsche, too, that I could zip around our sensible neighborhood in?"

"Sure, if that's what you want," she said. "Although I always saw you more as a heavy-duty pickup truck kind of guy."

"Is that what you want?" he asked.

"A pick-up truck?" She smirked. "Not exactly. But what if we could have all of that, would you be happy with me?"

He gazed into her eyes and leaned in for a kiss. "Anne, I'm happy with you right here where we are. I don't need a bunch of fancy things even if I could have them."

She pulled back. "Yes, but would you be happy with me somewhere else? Not here in the desert. In a lovely city."

"City?" He twisted his face. "You never said anything about a city. No thanks. I don't—"

"Suburbs. Not city. I meant something... a little more green."

"You aren't happy here, are you?" He leaned his head against the side of the barn. "Best to tell me now if the future we're planning together isn't one that you'll stick with."

She reached for his hand. "I'm not planning a future without you. I'm wondering if we could start a future together somewhere else."

"I'm sorry if I don't have the money for that, to give you a life like you used to have." He stood up and brushed off his jeans. "I won't ever have that kind of money."

"What if I did?" She froze, held her breath, and waited for his reaction.

"What are you talking about? What are you trying to say?" He squatted down next to her. "Anne, what's going on?"

She told him everything. He didn't speak, only sat down beside her and listened.

"I have a few more days before Ronnie reaches out to me," she said. "What should I do? What do I tell him?"

"That's not my job to say. I'm not about to tell you what to do with your money. You're an adult and can make up your own mind."

"Don't you care? What if I moved tomorrow back down to that huge house? Wouldn't you miss me?"

"I'm not gonna start playing the role of a jealous fiancé. I'm just me. I'm here. You decide where you want to be." He shook his head. "I can tell you right now that I won't be happy caged into a box like that."

"The house is huge."

"On a Cracker Jacks box lot. I'll go stir crazy. Montana, maybe. West LA, no."

"Why are you judging something that you know nothing about? Palatial homes, all custom-designed. You have no idea what it's like to live down there."

"Guess maybe I'm too country for you." Steve rose, stared at her for a moment and shook his head. He turned and trudged towards the orchard.

Anne said nothing. Simply watched him until his image shrank too small to distinguish from the dirt.

Why couldn't he be happy with the news? Anybody else would be thrilled with the opportunity. Why was Steve being so ungrateful and stubborn?

She wouldn't go chasing after him. She'd done nothing wrong. He's the one who should apologize to her for acting childish.

Anne sat there an hour, wallowing in self-pity. Maybe he was right. Maybe Steve was too country for her. If so, why did her heart ache?

Anne sat across the table from her grandpa during dinner, tearing pieces off her biscuit and putting them in her mouth without blinking.

"What's the matter, Anne?" her grandpa asked.

"Nothing." She tore off another piece of bread.

"I may be old, but I ain't stupid," he said. "What are you and Steve fussing about?"

"Who said we were fussing?"

He raised an eyebrow. "I wasn't born yesterday."

"Grandpa, if you could leave this ranch and move into a beautiful house alongside a lake for free, would you go?"

"We're not having this discussion again. With the pennies they're offering, I wouldn't have enough for a house at all, much less a beautiful one alongside a lake."

"But if you could?"

"Be a darn fool not to." He shoved a bite of pot roast into his mouth and leaned back in his chair, chewing slowly and deliberately, indicating there'd be no further questions.

She blinked hard. Had her grandpa agreed that he'd move to a lake if they offered him enough money to pay for it? Her brain ran wild with the possibilities. How could she weave the two men who meant the most to her into her plans for a better future?

The business cards. She smirked. Perhaps there was a way.

After morning chores were done and she had the house to herself, Anne slipped into the kitchen to make a call. She turned the dial on the rotary phone eleven times and waited.

A man with a slick voice picked up on the third ring.

"This is Andy Hoffman's granddaughter," Anne said. "I'd like to schedule a confidential meeting with you and your partner."

"You did what?" Steve said, raising his voice not out of surprise, not anger. "Are you kidding me? Why on earth?"

"Just hear me out, please," Anne said. "I've already talked to Ronnie, too."

Steve paced between the pear trees. "What is your grandpa going to say?"

"He's not to know." She crossed her arms. "You have to promise me that. The developers will write it into the contract that they'll give my grandpa the best lakefront house that they're going to build alongside the new man-made lake that will be stocked with fish. He can sit on a dock and fish all day if he wants."

"And he won't be suspicious?" he asked.

"He'll think he won from holding out for so long. In the contract, I've got a separate agreement for them to pay extra for his house. Ronnie is drafting it up for me. You and I will get a smaller place down the way a bit, maybe buy out the McGregory family. They never knew how to dig a proper well. We'll bring the horses and animals with us."

"Are you sure this is what you want?" Steve stopped and stood in front of her. His eyes held hers, searching. "This is a huge decision. It will change everyone's lives forever."

"For the best," she said. "And for once, I feel sure about it. This is what I want."

"You can't take this back. You understand what you're losing out on if you do this."

She nodded. "The sensible house in the sensible neighborhood."

He eyed her with suspicion. "What's worth giving all that up for?"

"I choose love and joy over delicate vases on delicate tables."

"In a sensible neighborhood," he added with a chuckle. He reached forward, cradled her head in his hands, and pulled her close for a kiss.

"Going to have a seat or you going to wear out a trail in the carpet?" Anne's grandpa asked her one evening. "Got some news for you."

Anne sat beside him on the couch. She bit her lower lip and waited. Best to act surprised.

"I made a deal," he said.

"About what?" Her pitch was too high. She lowered it. "What do you mean?"

"Don't get mad, but I talked it over with Steve, and he explained the plans you two made." He smiled. "The two of you planning to buy a couple of acres, down the way?"

She nodded, careful to avoid eye contact lest she rouse suspicion.

He sighed, leaned back, and crossed his hands behind his head. "Can't stop the inevitable. I'm getting older… Ranching is hard work… I mean sooner or later—"

"Are you selling?" She spared him from having to say the words.

"Are you disappointed?"

"Not if you got a better deal than they were offering."

"I did," he said. "If you and Steve would—"

"Take care of the animals? Glad to do it." She glanced over at him afraid to find regret in his eyes. Instead, contentment rested comfortably on his face.

"Going to finally get to do that fishing we kept talking about," he said.

She gave him a tight embrace. "I'm happy for you, Grandpa. You deserve it."

In the year that followed, a simple wedding ceremony on the ranch came and went, and the land development began. Her grandpa stayed in his old house while the orchard and fields were plowed under. The new barn was spared and rumor had it that at least one film company was interested in leasing it out for use as a movie set, in a strange nod to Anne's dad's past.

The new town was christened Lake Los Angeles, a grand name for a grand planned town near a new manmade lake. A gorgeous restaurant with a wooden spire was constructed on a pier where her grandpa spent some time fishing.

"I'm going to saddle up Sage and have a ride over there for one last look," Anne said, "before they knock down our old house."

"Are you sure?" Steve asked. "In your condition?"

"I'm pregnant, not dying." She rolled her eyes.

Sage led the way on the familiar path through the desert back home. They paused fifty yards away while a bulldozer broke down the gateway leading into the Hoffman Ranch.

It took her breath away to witness her old life disappearing. Had she made the right decision? A familiar shriek came from high overhead. There, against the clear blue sky, a hawk circled, keeping an eye on her.

"Don't worry," Anne said. "I won't throw any rocks at you this time." She placed her hand across her abdomen. "I'm done throwing rocks."

The hawk shrieked again and soared higher, riding the gusts of wind.

Sage's ears rotated and she whinnied.

Anne scratched the horse's neck and stared into the distance. Joshua trees dotted the fields beyond the development, beyond Lovejoy Buttes, where the desert remained untouched and wild. While her heart had been tamed, her spirit, like the desert wind, remained wild. Rather than fight change, it was braver for her to embrace it. She chose to have a say in the way things came to be rather than allow others to dictate how they'd be. Her dreams were rooted in reality, in what mattered most.

"Come on, Sage." Anne gently kicked her heels. "Let's head home."

Epilogue

Some stories are joyful and lighthearted—a welcome respite from the world; others are bittersweet and weighty—a mirror for many of us to self-reflect, to feel seen and heard and to process our own complicated emotions.

Andy and Anne's story is one of the latter. Andy got his house on the lake and even enjoyed his seventy-fifth birthday dinner at the fancy Mr. B's Restaurant, splurging on a bottle of wine pulled up from the wood-paneled wine cellar. Anne and Steve raised their three children together on their ranch alongside their chickens, horses, goats, and a few prized pigs. Every summer, they carried on the tradition of bringing hatching chicks to the fairgrounds. Steve even acquiesced to her wild idea of getting a pair of bison—a bit of Montana.

Anne found the peace she'd been seeking. She thanked the heavens that her grandpa didn't live long enough for his fears of developers destroying the land to come to fruition. In 1981, the lake went dry—it wasn't sealed properly and no amount of convincing could get everyone to agree on a tax increase to bring it back. The love and joy had drained from the earth, and Lake Los Angeles no longer had a lake.

Instead of leaving well enough alone, and allowing the neighborhood to fade away into oblivion, another developer settled in. Since the lake wasn't around anymore, the new investors doubled down, betting they could sell the dirt as affordable housing.

This new company set up shop in a little trailer with colorful rows of flags flapping in the wind along the nearby highways, leading like a runway to a fabulous destination.

Inside, glossy pictures mounted on foam boards displayed artist renderings of the possibilities. They advertised green grass, lush trees, gorgeous tile counters, and carpentry details, the windows and garage framed with painted trim. The salesperson showed naïve hopefuls around the beautiful model homes with the new carpet smell—Look at the fireplace! And all these windows!—then returned them back to the trailer office with the glorious air conditioning.

The AC was the trap. When they went inside, they didn't want to go back out, so they temporarily hid from the heat and listened to the sales pitch until it sounded pretty darn good. They could pick out their lot. And these people here at this table could finance it. Just sign here.

So, the houses multiplied. Concrete foundations were poured up and down dirt roads, electric and telephone wires strung in from the bigger towns—lines haphazardly buried underground in the neighborhoods—water lines connected, and septic tanks buried in every backyard. Because you couldn't tell one tumbleweed from the next, they erected cheap chain-link fences around each one-acre plot.

Desert wind swept dirt across the foundations. Once the framing and stucco walls went up, the wind blew tumbleweeds around the houses—and the dirt always found a way in.

Another real estate company set up camp on the opposite end of the community in a race to see who could build faster. And in this way, the two developers built competing homes, some on the same streets. In the spirit of this two-sided competition, Lake Los Angeles became an anomaly, a single town, yet a twin town, split down the middle, eventually each with its own zip code, one tied to Palmdale, the other tied to Lancaster.

In 1984, Kiara's mom, Marcy Leneghan, bought one of the first houses on the Palmdale side in a new neighborhood below Lovejoy Butte, on the other side of the dry lake bed. Newly divorced, she drove her two young children Kiara and Tommy two hours east, through the mountain pass and across the desert to visit as the house was built in stages—the foundation: Here's where our house will stand!—the wood framing: This is going to be the kitchen!—the asphalt shingle roof: It's almost done now!—the windows: That's your room, Kiara! And this one's yours, Tommy!—and the driveway, where their Dodge Colt was parked.

Maybe, Marcy kept telling herself, if she kept up the enthusiasm, she'd eventually feel something other than emptiness and dread.

Six-year-old Kiara, on the other hand, had no enthusiasm, only dread....

Read more in *Dare to Dream*, Kiara's story!

Author's Note

I hope you've enjoyed Anne's story! *Sway with the Wind* is the prequel novella to the *Desert of Dreams Series*. The rest of the books in the *Desert of Dreams Series* are standalone full-length novels. They tell inspiring stories for survival amidst difficult family and desert landscapes during the 1980s and 90s in the Antelope Valley. With duplicate timelines and connected characters, each book tells a different friend's story. When you read *Dare to Dream (Desert of Dreams Series Book 1)* and *Reach for Hope (Desert of Dreams Series Book 2),* look for hidden references to this prequel!

What was the inspiration behind this series?

    The tagline of the *Desert of Dreams Series* says it all: Trauma. Resilience. Hope. Everyone has their own story.
    Growing up, I didn't know many people who had "normal" childhoods. Most of my friends, much like my characters, survived trauma that presented itself in many forms—neglect, as well as physical, mental, emotional, and sexual abuse.
    While being a latchkey kid may have been typical in the 1980s and 1990s, abuse and neglect should never be normalized. Ever. It's amazing how a great psychologist, counselor, or therapist can help people work through trauma and develop resilience, so that we can overcome the worst of the worst. Keep hope alive, because as my friends will tell you: it does get better. And there are good people out there. Trust me... there are. Hold on to those friendships.

Acknowledgements

A million thanks to my artistic and supportive husband Leo who encouraged me when life became heavy. A writer couldn't ask for a better partner and alpha reader. Fun fact: he drew the hawk that appears on each chapter page!

A huge thank you to Peggy Ronning, Museum Curator III, at the California Historic Park's Antelope Valley Indian Museum for guidance during my research which helped me to find the lake. I was incredulous that the name I conjured (logically of course with the proximity to Lovejoy Buttes) was the real name. I appreciate your help locating USGS and other topographic maps from the early twentieth century, which eluded me despite hours of web searches and scouring databases. To Retired LA County Fire Captain Mike Aplanalp: no amount of research can replace the experience gained over a lifetime of dedicated firefighting. Thank you for helping me to realistically portray the flames on Andy's ranch and successfully douse them. Thank you to Fiona Jayde Media: I love how the cover design captures the essence of the story. Many, many thanks to my editor Jennifer Silva Redmond for your editing expertise. This story is better because of your guidance with both the content and line edits.

Jenny Orci, Ken Elliott, and Maria Leighton: thank you for your helpful feedback and encouragement. A special thanks to Dionne Veselko for your enthusiastic support.

Lastly, thank you to my readers: I love hearing from every single one of you—sharing your personal connections to my stories means the world to me. I hope you continue to enjoy the rest of the books in this *Desert of Dreams Series*.

Discussion Questions

1. Have you ever had to deal with grief? If so, how did you handle it? What are healthy versus unhealthy coping mechanisms?

2. What are warning signs of depression or anxiety? When should you seek help?

3. When faced with difficult decisions, how do you determine the best course of action? Do you rely on logic or emotions?

4. How do you react to mistakes you've made? Is there anything you wish you could undo?

5. How do you react to change? In what ways can you better adapt to things you cannot change?

6. How can we build resilience to overcome life's challenges?

7. What are your dreams in life? What do you hope to achieve? What steps can you take to get there?

If you or someone you know is struggling with their mental health or is in crisis, please reach out for help. In the US, you can call or text the National Suicide and Crisis Lifeline at **988**.

About the Author

For thirteen years, Amanda LaPera grew up in the small rural community of Lake Los Angeles, where, much like her characters, she was disappointed to learn there wasn't a lake and everything she planted died. She and her friends survived, buoyed by resilience and determination. Now her hobbies include watching hummingbirds in her yard surrounded by trees, playing board games with her husband, taunting her sons, and appeasing her dogs. She has sworn off succulents, because she believes they belong in the desert.

Amanda LaPera is a national award-winning author. Her book, *Losing Dad, Paranoid Schizophrenia: A Family's Search for Hope*, won a Silver IBPA Award, was a *BookLife Prize* quarter finalist and a *Readers' Favorite* Awards finalist. Her sequel *Finding Dad, Paranoid Schizophrenia: An End to the Search* was a finalist in the IAN *Book of the Year Awards*. She teaches English and is a member of the California Writers Club and the Southern California Writers Association.

She is working on her *Desert of Dreams* young adult series, set during the 1980s and 90s in the California High Desert. To be notified of new releases and special deals, sign up for her newsletter at **www.amandalapera.com**.

FB.com/amandalapera　　Amanda LaPera　　@desertstoryteller
FB.com/desertofdreamsbook

Also by the Author

Fiction

Desert of Dreams Series: Coming-of-age standalone books connected by friendship, time, and place. Surviving difficult family amidst a small-town landscape during the 1980s and 90s.

Sway with the Wind: A Prequel Novella (Desert of Dreams Series)
Anne's story takes place 20 years earlier!

Dare to Dream (Desert of Dreams Series Book 1)
Kiara's story

Reach for Hope (Desert of Dreams Series Book 2)
Carolyn's story

Embrace the Truth (Desert of Dreams Series Book 3)
Misty's story

Allow in Light (Desert of Dreams Series Book 4) - Nicole's story coming soon!

Mend the Heart: The Final Story (Desert of Dreams Series Book 5) - Jenny's story coming soon!

Nonfiction

Psychology Memoir: A poignant true story of how a father's sudden late-onset mental illness and homelessness impact his family.

Losing Dad, Paranoid Schizophrenia: A Family's Search for Hope (10th Anniversary Edition)

Finding Dad, Paranoid Schizophrenia: An End to the Search (the sequel)

To order books:

www.ingramcontent.com/pod-product-compliance
Lightning Source LLC
LaVergne TN
LVHW040101080526
838202LV00045B/3726